Immortal by Magic

Thorne Sisters Chronicles
Book Three

RENEE JOINER

Oshun
Publications

Book design by MMB

Published by Oshun Publications

www.oshunpublications.com

Contents

Did you know you can take every story with you?

I know it's tough these days to simply find the time to relax and curl up with a good book. This is why I'm delighted to share that I have books available in audio book format.

Best of all, you can get the audio book version of any book by me for free as part of a 30-day Audible trial.

Members get free audio books every month and exclusive discounts. It's an excellent way to explore and determine if audio book learning works for you.

If you're not satisfied, you can cancel anytime within the trial period. You won't be charged, and you can even keep your audio book.

To choose a free audio book, click on your favorite title's cover to be taken to Audible's website for details.

Remember, there's no obligation to buy.

reneejoinerauthor.com/audiobooks

JOIN MY NEWSLETTER

GET UPDATES, FREEBIES & GIVEAWAYS

RENEEJOINERAUTHOR.COM/NEWSLETTER

Prologue

PROLOGUE: 1682

Her footsteps clinked against the cold marble as Morgan walked, her high heels echoing loudly in the otherwise brisk hall. The chamber was open to the courtyard, and the mist of her breath wafted behind her. Chill from the early spring weather bit at her skin, but she refused to close the cloak around her.

To her right, Zachariah Miller was tending to the fire, his black, mangy hair drifting in the breeze. He sniffed loudly and rubbed a hand across his nose.

As Morgan continued to walk, he was occasionally obscured by the hedges that had remained somewhat uncared for. Still, she stared over at him suspiciously.

"Why don't you stop walking so much and actually come to see me?" he asked, not looking back at her.

The clinking of her boots fell silent as she stopped, still staring at him. "I didn't know if you wanted to be disturbed."

"If I wasn't disturbed before, I am now," he said, finally turning to see her. "You look cold. Come visit me by the fire." Zachariah beckoned to her and gestured to a damp log on his right.

Morgan strode over to him, adjusted her skirts, and then sat down on the log. She could feel the wood's dampness seeping through the cotton threads. Putting a hand on the log, she allowed red energy to slowly flow through her fingers, sending a stream of steam from the log to warm her backside. Morgan glanced up at him with a curt smile.

"So," he said, finally turning his gaze away from her and back to the fire, "what now, on our quest?"

"What do you mean?" she asked, pulling at her big sleeves.

"They kicked us out of London—or rather, you did. We could have stayed at the court for another few years if you hadn't tipped off the magistrate by magically adjusting your skirts."

"He only supposed me to be a witch. He didn't have any evidence."

Zachariah harrumphed under his breath.

Morgan let out a sigh. "If it wasn't for your need for comfort, we wouldn't be in this mess in the first place. We could have stayed in Northern Ireland for another century or more. As it is, we'll be lucky if we aren't burnt at the stake in the next few years."

"Don't worry about that," Zachariah said, suddenly grinning. He stood and stretched, still wearing the clothes of an aristocrat with the leggings and the pompously large, regal jacket, despite their banishment to Scotland. "I've got a plan."

Morgan rolled her eyes and leaned her head back. "You've always got a plan."

"This one is real, though. For once, we can stay in whatever spot we want, for as long as we want. All we need to do is find the Stone of Obscuras."

She lowered her head quickly and stared at him, mouth agape. "You're not serious. We have no business looking for the Stone. For all you know, it could tear us apart, not save us. What do you think you're playing at?"

"Think about it," he went on, sitting down next to her and seizing a plant shaft. He started to draw in large concentric circles, all based around the barest of pebbles he found next to the fire. "The legend says that the Stone of Obscuras can be used to store the powers of those around it. The Stone is said to have enough power to increase the quality of life and magic of those who wield it. If we get our hands on it, we could, I don't know, become invincible!"

Morgan watched him as he stood and stared up at the sky. "Why would we want that?"

"Why... Morgan, you can't be serious. After all the time you've spent trying to blend in, constantly terrified should you be caught, it seems to me you would be the most willing to go after something like this."

She stood and turned her back to him, staring at the ground. "I just don't want to hurt people."

"Morgan," he said, turning her to face him. "Come on now. It's not about that. Gaining more power is never about that. It's always about staying alive. Think about the last time you wanted to stay in one place. Whether in the hills of Scotland or the planes of Ireland, there's always something stopping us from sticking around. Can you imagine it? We'd never have to run again. We could find a home in America, away from everything else. We don't have to use it for evil, only to keep us safe." He grinned at her, taking her hand.

"Neither of your sisters, Brenna nor Alaina, has to suffer forever. In fact, they could join us, and we wouldn't have to worry about this ever again. We can be on our own, finally." He was giddy, throwing his hands in the air. "Can't you just imagine it?"

Morgan's eyes were fixed on him; he had an aura about him that troubled her. He seemed oblivious of her reaction, however, for he pulled her to her feet and began to twirl her about, finally raising her into the air, staring into her eyes, and holding her there for several minutes.

"Let me down," she insisted, trying to act jubilantly but failing.

He lowered her, a look of concern on his face. "Is there something wrong?" Zachariah pleaded with her with his eyes. They seemed to cloud slightly, so she smiled at him.

"Of course not."

He beamed, grabbing her by the waist and dipping her, her red hair near the fire.

"Be careful," she squealed, quickly grasping at the endangered locks. But when she saw his face, she couldn't help but laugh herself. To be free, she thought. What a concept.

Zachariah's eyes were glued to the map in front of him. Every so often, he would glance up for just a moment only to look back down and stare at the drawing again. "We must be nearing it," he said, almost to himself. "It says here on the map that there should be a rock face up ahead, and below that, there must be the entrance to the cave. Do you see it?"

Morgan had been busy flattening the folds of her dress with a hand and gazing up at the sky, which promised rain. "I'm sorry, what?"

"The cave," Zachariah repeated impatiently. "Do you see it?"

She dropped her eyes to the cliff face and scanned the area. "No."

"Use your magic."

"Why use mine? You're the one looking for it. I'm still not certain about the entire thing."

"Morgan, my love," he said, lowering the map and running a hand around her waist. "We are doing this for each other. We'll be able to keep each other safe if we locate the stone. It'll be like a new lease on life. We could spend the years together simply roaming the lands of the Americas and never worry about anyone finding us. We could be completely impervious to the ravages of time."

He was rambling again, and Morgan looked over at him with some suspicion before staring at the ground. The sense of unease in her gut made her think twice about finding the Stone, but the look in his eyes suggested that she was being silly. She felt guilty. Her trepidation seemed a sort of betrayal to Zachariah. After all, he was doing this for them.

"Here," he said, magic emitting from his hands. She felt the rush of warmth emanating through her body. "I know you've been cold on this trip. Maybe a little warmth is just what we need before we start looking. It looks like it might rain. Do we have that tent?"

Morgan nodded her eyes still downcast. She rummaged through her pocket purse to pull out the tent. They laid it out and crawled inside just as the first droplets began to fall.

She hadn't said a word in over an hour when she turned to him. "What is it in America that you want to see?"

He laid back, staring at the roof of the tent. "I want to see it all. The huge rivers, the grand mountains. Can you imagine living in a place like that, so far from here, where we don't have to worry about who everyone is? We will be completely on our own, just you and me. We'll be in the wilds of the west, and we can forget everything else."

"They wouldn't try to kill us if we didn't have magic. Maybe we could give it up."

He sat up, then, staring at her with a furrowed brow. "Give it up? Are you insane? If we're without immortality, what's the point of living? Think of all the wonders we could see, all the technology that has yet to be discovered."

"I rather like the way things are. I find it peaceful living in the countryside. We don't have to worry about growing food since our magic will care for that. We don't have to worry about neighbors if we live far enough away from everyone. We can live in tranquil bliss."

He laughed. "You have crazy ideals, Morgan. That's part of the reason why I'm in love with you. You're so simple."

She frowned slightly, and then turned onto her side.

In the morning, the sun shone in rays through the disappearing rain clouds. Morgan packed up the tent and stuffed it back into her pocket purse. She sighed in resignation as she watched Zachariah return to the map, sitting cross-legged on the ground.

"Let's just start walking," she suggested. "We're bound to come across it sooner or later. There's no point in staring at it for another three days."

He threw her a look of an annoyance, then quickly stood and dusted off his trousers. "Very well." Zachariah strode toward the cliff without her.

Annoyed, Morgan walked several feet behind him, gazing around at the mountainside. A pine marten scrambled up a tree, sending a flock of crossbills careening into the air. A badger wandered lazily across the wilderness, not caring about their intrusion.

Finally, they reached the sheer, gray rock face. Its craggy surface hardly seemed the ideal location for a cave.

Still, Zachariah stalked to its surface and laid a hand on it, chthonic magic radiating from his hands.

"Well, aren't you going to help me?" he asked after several minutes.

Fighting a heightened sense of unease, Morgan hesitantly shuffled toward the rock and laid a hand on it. She closed her eyes. The outline of the bluff gave way to geometric renderings. She could see the solid outline of the rock for miles until...

There was a divot in the long stretch of solidness.

"Here," she said, still not opening her eyes. "I think I found it."

"Very good," Zachariah said, jumping toward her. "That's my little peach blossom." He pinched her on the cheek, hard.

Morgan rubbed the injury and continued to walk toward the entrance. It was massive. The gray rock's foreboding exterior made her grit her teeth in anxiety. She stared up and down the broad face, knowing the entrance was just ahead of her but afraid to take further steps.

"Well, where is it?" Zachariah was once again at her side, staring with her.

"It's here." Morgan reached her hand forward into the gray rock, her hand disappearing.

Zachariah gave a whoop and walked headlong into the boundary.

Inside lay a vast lake, shimmering blue. Along the sides of the cavern were torches with green flames, and the smell of sulfur and sage filled the air. In the center of the lake was a platform, no more than a few feet across. Ahead of them lay a boat, still as sin on the water's surface. The green lights grew brighter as they continued toward the boat, and soon the lake seemed filled to the brim with the eerie glow.

"Come on, then," Zachariah said, hopping into the boat and bidding her to follow.

"Zachariah," she said in little more than a squeak, "Zachariah, I'm not so sure about all this. It seems wrong, somehow. We should go back."

"Wrong? We have traveled all this way to find this Stone. Don't tell me you're giving up now. We could have a beautiful life together if you'd only trust me on this."

"Can't we have a life without this? We don't need a stone of power to be happy. We could settle in America, raise some children, and live our own lives. We have immortality if that's what you want."

"Children? What makes you think I could be a family man, Morgan? We've been together for nearly five years now. You should know I've never had that intention. I simply want to be left alone, and this Stone could do it for us. We could be at the pinnacle of our powers if you would just trust me. We could be unstoppable. Imagine the power we would have if you would simply trust that this is the best thing for both of us."

Morgan's uneasiness turned into sour anger. "I'm not stepping on that boat. If you want to live a life with that Stone and without me, be my guest, but there is something evil here."

She was bluffing. He'd come back to her, she knew it. It was only one of his vain imaginations that assumed that they would be king and queen of the world. Where would he be without her? She had the years and the magic on her side. If he wanted power, he couldn't do it without her.

They stared at each other for what seemed to be an eternity before he sank down into the boat and pushed off with an oar.

Screams of betrayal pounded in her ears. Her face went white as she saw him rowing toward the platform in the center of the cavern. "What are you doing? Come back!"

He said nothing, rowing passionately, his strokes becoming more vigorous with every strike of his oars to the water. He paddled with fervor. Had it not been for the escalating brightness of the room, Morgan might not have seen the glisten of sweat on his arms, the massive shake of his locks as he continued with effort.

Once he reached the other side, he leaped to the platform without bothering to secure the boat, though there was no need in the still waters. He didn't look back or call out to her. He only drew nearer the Stone. Though far away, Morgan could see his eyes blazing a color she had not seen on him before. She caught her breath as he reached for the Stone.

A whirlwind of air struck him from behind. His chthonic magic whirled about him in a blaze of darkening fire. Dark tendrils of black ooze overtook his body and swirled him end over end. He was held captive in the onslaught of black energy filling his soul and erupting out of his mouth, nose, and ears.

There were no screams but her own as she called out his name. She was desperate, intent on freeing him from his prison though having no power to do so. She sent out a wave of red magic, finally hitting him in the chest. He froze in midair. The black ooze that had enveloped his body halted and, like a vacuum, pulled itself back into him with a low rumble. He fell to the platform in a heap, not moving.

Morgan stood at the far end of the lake, her hands still held out in a conjuring stance. She waited for several minutes before she called his name. "Zachariah?"

No response.

"Zachariah!" she tried again, screaming.

Finally, he lifted his head and stared over at her. She held back a scream as she looked at his body, doused in ebony. He drifted over to her limply, going without the boat altogether. His feet were mere inches from the water, but still, he floated, as though no longer human. He continued to dangle over to her until he was only a foot away.

Sick to her stomach, Morgan fought against the impulse to run by reaching a hand out to him. His body seemed to warp as she drew near. After a moment, his head lifted to face hers, and blackness covered the whites of his eyes. He grinned in a crazed fashion, his head tilting to the side. His black hair fell in damp ringlets over his face.

"Hello, Morgan," he said quietly.

"What's... what's happened to you?"

Though he seemed to hear, he kept the impossibly broad grin on his face without saying a word. Finally, he opened his mouth, and a long, black tongue emerged. He moved it in front of his face for a moment before stretching it further to lick her face, like sandpaper against her delicate skin.

Morgan stepped back in fear, though not daring to wipe the beast's saliva from her face. "Who are you?" she asked tremulously.

The black tongue returned to his mouth, and his lips spread impossibly wide. "We are Zachariah." It sounded as though two voices were speaking as one, Zachariah's familiar one combined with an incredibly low snarl. Zachariah dropped to his feet, his body was still limp. He raised a hand behind him, and the Stone shot to him.

"Of course, you are," Morgan said, trying not to show the fear she felt. "Zachariah, my love."

The creature's grin widened further. The creature's

smile broadened also. He managed to take a faltering step toward her, and she stepped away. "Morgan," it said. He continued to walk forward as if on broken legs held together only by magic.

She stepped away further, reaching for the entrance of the bluff with hands slicked with sweat.

"Why are you afraid?" the beast asked, taking more significant steps toward her. "We have what we've always wanted. A chance for both of us."

Morgan felt the waving fabric of magic behind her and took an additional step, landing outside the cavern. She ran.

"Don't run from me!" roared a voice behind her. She didn't look back; too afraid of what she might see. Instead, she scrambled off of the rock and ran through the moors, raising her skirts as she fled.

A blast of magic hit her from behind, and she fell to the ground in a skid. She rubbed at her back and felt something sticky. When she brought it to her face, she had to hold her breath to keep from gagging. It was black ooze, with faint traces of the chthonic magic that was usually Zachariah's color. As she continued to stare, the chthonic was consumed by the black and began to seep into her pores.

With a burst of energy, Morgan torched the black ooze from her skin, lighting her whole body aflame. Behind her came the sound of crunching bones, and she turned to see Zachariah running toward her, legs still twisted as though broken.

Finally, he was upon her. "You didn't think I could let you go that easily, did you? No, you're far too valuable to me." He reached out a hand, black protruding trailing in jagged daggers from his fingertips.

Morgan stared at him in horror. Summoning all her

power, she screamed, sending her magic as shrapnel toward him. He groaned and lay in a heap, red flame emitting from his body.

After a moment, however, he stood. His grin had been replaced by a long scowl, his stretched lips dripping from the look. He stumbled forward, reaching for her with his hands. She took a step back and stared at him. He began to drip black ooze all about him.

Morgan drew her magic in again, this time chanting a spell of invisibility, and saw her own shimmering body disappear as he reached for her. She ran, then, hearing only the frustrated cry from Zachariah echoing behind her.

ONE

It Begins

A straight and narrow road, nestled deep in the rolling mountains, caves, and other splendors of nature, crept between knotty roots of the enormous trees that bordered either side. Far from the reaches of dense human existence, maples, oaks, aspens, and elms rose to a dense canopy, forming a transient blanket over the town. During the fall, the countryside converted into a painted canvas of color. Bright crimson, orange, and golden foliage emerged during a final celebration before the cold dark winter ensued, transitioning to bare tree limbs that reached upward in a pitiful plea, begging for a reprieve of spring.

Along the byway, there were breaks of sun, illuminating bright sections of the faded grey pavement. It constructed an illusory path both for those that came and went into the rural community through this single lane.

The road zigzagged as it approached the populous. Splitting just past a sign announcing the arrival to Summer Avenue, along with the quirky slogan that boldly stated, "Not the end of the world, but you can see it from here."

The left junction continued along the north midline of the mountain, the first turn leading to a dead end street rising sharply up a hilly slope. The main stretch curved onward before branching into numerous side routes where two-story homes were squarely positioned in the middle of generous yards. The houses were a mix of neutral white Colonials, Victorians, and Cape Cods, most having monotonous black shutters with an occasional variation of grey or green.

The exteriors were simple but maintained, aside from the occasional porch needing a fresh coat of paint due to the harsh winter last year taking a toll on the wooden structures. Lilac trees and rhododendrons adorned the lawns, providing makeshift borders to property lines, replacing the need for fences.

The primary road, Second Street, continued for about a mile, winding past a variety of churches and an abandoned playground. At the end, by the brick high school, a large football field overlapped a baseball diamond, displaying a weathered blue and white scoreboard. The road extended right, circling past the sports park to a four-way intersection under a blinking yellow caution traffic light. Ironically was located adjacent to a dilapidated garage with several cars waiting for repair and piles of auto parts cluttering the small corner lot.

Entering the town via the south fork of Front Street, the road sloped down to the business section of the village, passing a natural spring. It followed the railroad tracks along storefronts such as the hardware, library, and grocery. A hard left at the divided crossroad would return to Second Street, passing a post office and gas station. Another looped road off to the right crossed over the single bridge spanning the river and rose up the lake, where summer months entailed moonlight swims from restless teenagers.

This town was a simple place; the seasons changed more than the people. Time was preserved, and the trees surrounding the valley created reassurance of seclusion. It was a place where family names spanned centuries, and neighbors knew each other's histories. Many were friendly, gossiping about the residents' happenings, while others preferred to remain loners and keep to themselves.

This is the town Morgan built with the coven. A haven for those persecuted for their magic. We got a feeling of "tribe" going, our own vibe and culture. Everyone was always welcome to visit, with the one B and B available for weary travelers. Those were the times magic was kept to a minimum.

For now, a small portion set up camp 10 miles in. A battle was coming and those who would survive will need their homes when they returned.

Morgan opened the locket containing her sisters' picture. It had been so long since she had seen them, nearly 300 years. It was simply a matter of time before they returned. Once they did, their reunion was cut short. The threat of Zachariah had started growing greater every day. She could sense the shift in magic as his powers grew. It was only a matter of time, she knew before he showed up at her doorstep.

Feeling Alaina beginning to stir, Morgan gestured to one of the witches in her coven to prepare a light meal. It was only weeks ago Alaina emerged from a coma patient. She still needed to take it slow.

Morgan breathed a sigh, staring out into the wooded surroundings. Bright lights flickered in golds, greens, reds, purples, and blues, sending shoots of color into the sky. Each new spell licked the edge of the shield, the bright blue of the barrier only visible when struck. They were just warming up.

Morgan tossed a smile back at her sister, Alaina, one of the few witches not engaged in setting up protections for their coven. She seemed deeply engrossed in The Alchemy. Its name was a bit deceptive since it also contained spells for protection, binding, attack, and the like. Each turn of the massive pages resulted in a puff of dust.

Of course, Alaina had only been in the camp for a couple of weeks. She was no doubt still tired from the recovery of the body she now inhabits. The woman before her, Lindsey, was in an accident where only her body survived. It had been so long since Morgan had seen Alaina and Brenna, and she knew they were together through their magic. Ever since Zachariah had become more powerful, it was more difficult to stay under his radar as he continued to want to kill them all at once.

A man approached. Jayden. He edged over with half a smile.

Morgan glanced over at him with a returning smile but then quickly looked away again, scratching at her nose with a sleeved arm.

He smiled, trying to catch her eye, running a hand through his brown hair. Morgan could feel his gaze on her, but she didn't give him more than an occasional glance. She sniffed, watching red sparks shooting from her fingertips.

"Hey," he said quietly. Suddenly, he was closer, reaching a hand out to touch her upper arm. He seemed to think better of it, and then slowly lowered it back to his side.

Morgan turned to stare at him for the first time, blue eyes flickering. She said nothing.

"I could help you know, do what I can?"

"No," she said under her breath. "No." Yellow and purple lights flickered across his face, the fading sunlight casting an unusual shadow. He was frowning slightly, but it was more than that. It was an expression of fear. Perhaps shame. "Thank you, Jayden, but there's really not a lot to do. There's enough firewood, food. I think the majority of the work is for the rest of us." She hazarded a smile, but it was weak.

She watched him walk away. He was in love with her, had been for some time. But he was mortal.

The face of the young boy shone in the flickering light of the flames. His village was set ablaze. Tears trickled down his young face as he looked up at her with those enormous, brown eyes. He wouldn't move.

Morgan kneeled down and placed a hand on his shoulder. "I'm sorry," she said, almost in a whisper.

The outlines of the dead flashed in and out of view. There was no moon; the only light came from the houses burning around them. Screams echoed in the distance. Gurgled noises. Abrupt stops. The town crumbled, silencing the voices of the dying with each crash from the breaking walls.

Sibyl called to Morgan, and she turned slightly, keeping a hand on the boy. "We've got to leave. Zachariah will be coming back. it's only a matter of time."

She had to shout above the din. Sienna-orange light erupted from her hands as she held back the crumbling of a house, threatening to crush several other witches. Morgan's copper hair flicked wildly about her face.

The house next to them sent up sparks as it began to collapse. A support beam cracked ominously, and Morgan glanced up at the house. She stood and grabbed the boy's upper arm, gently tugging. "We've got to go."

He pointed solemnly at several mounds on the ground. Morgan turned slowly, fearing the worst.

A pile of corpses lays in the direction the boy pointed. Only the infrequent flash of light from the flames illuminated what she saw.

A man, a woman, and two young girls lay on the ground, their faces darkened. The man was sprawled in front of the others. Arms burned in a position of pleading, staying in their place only by the crackling of burned flesh. The woman was face down, her arms across the two young girls. One girl lay with a dagger through her heart, still glowing red from the magic within. The other girl, barely a toddler, was almost completely hidden from view, encircled by the arms of her dead mother.

Morgan turned back to the boy, her mouth still open in amazement. A tear slipped down the child's face, leaving a trail through the dust that coated his cheeks. The house began to crumble.

"What's your name?" she asked, hazarding a smile and only partially succeeding. Though no sound came, he mouthed the name Jayden. "Jayden, eh?" He nodded.

Another supporting beam broke, sending a shower of sparks down on them. Morgan lifted a hand. A wave of red, translucent light erupted from her fingers, forming a shield around them both.

"Listen to me, Jayden," she said through labored breaths. "I'm sorry they're gone. You'll have to rely on me now, okay?"

Another tear streaked down his face, but he offered an almost imperceptible nod.

Morgan smiled. "Good. Don't worry now. I'll take care of you. We just have to move, all right?"

As she began to tug, the boy seemed to be made of wood. He made a gulping sound deep in his throat, loud enough to be heard above the rumbling of the fire blazing about them.

"Come on now. Don't be afraid. You'll join us. You'll be safe." Morgan smiled again, straining slightly from holding the magic field in check. A log from the house fell from the roof, colliding with her protection field and emitting a screaming pitch. She shuddered slightly but held on, removing her hand from his arm for just a moment to push back at the falling structure with both hands.

An enormous creak sounded as she put all her strength into shoving the house to the side. As the magic faded from her hands, she grabbed Jayden by the hand and started to run.

"Morgan." Alaina was waving a hand in front of her face, snapping her fingers occasionally. "Come out of it. You look like you're in a stupor."

Morgan blinked, and then faced Alaina. "Yes, sorry. Just lost in thought, I guess." She glanced over at Jayden, who had loosened his baggy white shirt to more easily chop wood. His back was to her.

Alaina let out a sigh and looked around. Hands on hips, she surveyed the surroundings. "It might hold against Zachariah. What do you think?"

"I wouldn't dare tell the others, but I'm not sure this is going to be enough. There's so much to consider, and Zachariah seems to be getting stronger all the time. There's no telling how powerful he might be now." Morgan bit her bottom lip. "But, I guess it'll have to do until Brenna gets back." She glanced over at Jayden again.

Alaina stepped in front of her, a smirk on her face.

"What?"

"I see the way he looks at you. He's been doing it for some time now." Morgan tried to roll her eyes, but Alaina slapped her playfully on the arm. "I'm serious. He's changed quite a bit since he was a boy—he's no longer that cowering child you found amidst that ruin. He's grown up. Why not give him a chance?"

"No!" Morgan said, more forcefully than she had intended.

Alaina looked slightly taken aback but recovered quickly.

Morgan gave a half-hearted snort. "You know how it is. He's mortal. Besides, it's been a while since we've had a good herbalist, and he's been studying for years. I'd hate to let that go now. It's hard to find someone without magic willing to spend his time with a coven, and going down that road might just send him away."

"True, but you've been in love with mortals before."

"And each time, I swore it was the last. But I mean it this time. I can't bear to see another die, not when I can keep a steady head." The wind had whipped a strand of red hair across her face, covering her expression.

Her heart ached for those she had lost. Samuel. Beau. Kian. They each had left scars. Samuel had died of old age in her arms. Beau had left for another woman when he saw himself growing old while she hadn't aged a day. Kian. He had died young, at the hands of Zachariah. Just another reason to hate that warlock.

"You could give it up, you know."

Morgan turned to her sister. Breathing out an incredulous scoff, she said, "My immortality? Can you only imagine how Zachariah would decimate us? He would kill me first, and then come after you and Brenna. It would only be a matter of time before he overtook this place and either added the coven we've worked so hard to preserve to his horde or killed them in a matter of days. I can't take that chance, and you know it."

"What? you think that Brenna and I couldn't do it without you? That you have all the powers and where-withal to take him down?"

Morgan sighed, eyes closing and head falling behind her. After a moment, she looked back at her sister. "Of course not. You know that I have every confidence in you. But think about it. We are stronger as a group. If Zachariah takes down even one of us, we might not be strong enough to beat him. We weren't the last time."

"Kian," Morgan said under her breath, seeing the pain in his eyes

as he knelt before Zachariah, a dagger to his throat. She dared do nothing but stand still. Even her breath caught.

Zachariah grinned in pleasure, his piercing blue eyes like ice into her soul. "Oh. Is this yours?" He lifted the dagger, causing a stream of blood to leak down the side of Kian's neck. Kian did nothing. He only knelt, breathing shallowly and staring directly into Morgan's eyes. "What a pity."

Morgan lowered her hands; the red glow faded into nothing. All around her were the screams from her coven, the echoing blasts, the pleading of the doomed. She might have done it. She might have made Zachariah suffer, if not for his knowledge of her love. As it was, he stood with that wicked smile, punishing her with his fury.

"Call them off."

Morgan swallowed hard. She stood erect, forgoing her stance to not betray her intentions. "Sibyl!"

The fighting ceased for a moment, and there was a deathly silence. The sound of Brenna's footsteps on the forest floor sounded thunderous in the deafening quiet. It finally stopped as Sibyl stood by her side.

"Call them off."

Through the corner of her eye, Morgan saw Sibyl nod once, holding up a hand. The coven started to retreat.

Morgan sucked in her breath as she stared at Kian, tears coming to her eyes. His black hair whipped gently in the wind, and his own eyes began to tear slightly. He bit his lip, and then offered a weak smile.

It was then that Zachariah slit his throat.

"No!" Morgan screamed, reaching out a hand in desperation. Zachariah's black Ring began to strike as Kian fell to the ground, dead. She fell to her knees, staring into his dark eyes, which remained open as blood gushed from his wound.

Someone was pulling at her. It all seemed like a dream. The fog of her tears clouded everything. Distant explosions erupted around her. Zachariah was running in slow motion. Sibyl was casting spells in *succession, though they seemed to freeze in midair. Everything turned black.*

Alaina's face went sour, but before she could turn to leave, a scream echoed through the trees. Both Morgan and Alaina jumped, turning to see a witch of their coven stumbling toward them. Every breath seemed labored.

"Sibyl, what—" But Morgan stopped mid-sentence, suddenly seeing a purple wisp slowly seeping from her side. A brass knife was protruding from the wound with his inscription branded to the hilt of the blade: Zachariah.

Sibyl removed the hand covering her side to reveal a gash, her magic draining out in a pool on the ground. "It's Zachariah."

TWO

The Disciple

MORGAN'S HEART DROPPED. WITHOUT EVEN A GLANCE AT Alaina, she started in the direction Sibyl had come, her eyes set straight ahead. She didn't look over at the wood-pile as she called out, "Jayden, tend to Sibyl. Do what you can for her."

Jayden started, and then ran after Morgan. "What is it?" He had to practically jog to keep up with her pace.

"Sibyl says it's Zachariah. He's here. That's impossible, of course. He would have had to walk through my personal spells to make it. It must be someone else, someone working for him, perhaps." Her commentary was no longer directed at Jayden, only an endless stream of thoughts. "Seth is in command under Zachariah if the intelligence is correct." She struck her forehead in anger. "Of course."

Her pace quickened, and Jayden laid a hand on her shoulder, trying to slow her down. "I don't understand," he said. "Getting through those barriers is impossible."

Finally, she stopped, turning to him in a fit of rage. "Did I not say to take care of Sibyl? We cannot lose another witch in this battle." Morgan stared at him, her nostrils flared, and her mouth set in a thin line.

"Do you care nothing for her life?"

"Did you not hear me? You must heal her!"

"Oh, I heard you," he said, his face starting to flush. "All you want is another witch to fuel this fire between you and Zachariah. Her life means nothing more than another pair of hands in the war."

Morgan breathed deeply, staring icily at him. "You should hate him as much as I. Do you not remember that he killed your family?"

"I remember it daily. Still, think of the others here. Think of yourself."

Morgan walked up to him stiffly, her nose only inches from his own. "I will not have anyone else die at the hands of that murderer." She turned and continued to walk away.

"Morgan, wait," Alaina called after her, but she didn't turn. Alaina rushed to her side and put a hand on her shoulder. "Morgan, wait. Be reasonable. He can't have gotten through the barriers. You put some of them up yourself."

Morgan shrugged off her sister's hand and whirled on her heel to face Alaina. "Don't you think I know that? Sibyl is lying back there on the ground with a gash in her side. It has to be someone from his Dark Ring. It's only a matter of time before he comes."

Alaina's expression softened. "Even if he's here, you can't fight him alone."

"I won't be." And, for the first time in days, Morgan smiled and took her sister's hand. "I've got you, and Brenna is well on her way to full capacity. But I have to find out what is happening before it happens again."

Alaina nodded and returned the smile. "We're all each other's got, you know."

"I know, but I've still got my immortality. I'll be fine. With any luck, there won't be any more violence for a time. Just make sure you come as soon as Brenna wakes." She gave Alaina's hand an extra squeeze before releasing it. "You'll catch up."

Just then, a bang sounded in the distance. Morgan turned, suddenly fearful. She began to run, her long hair whipping behind her. Explosions of purple, green, orange, and black filled the lighting sky. Blasts shook the earth, causing Morgan to fall to her knees. She spread her hands and gripped the ground. She could feel her magic pulsing through her. Her own coven engaged with Zachariah's.

Leaping to her feet, she tore through the forest, racing to the beat of the booms. Her heartbeat thumped in her ears. Her hands splayed as she ran, trying to prevent the numbness that was coursing through her arms.

At last, she was there, her coven at the forefront, Seth and his Dark Ring striking with resulting blows. Red magic blazed from her fingers, and she lifted her arm to set off a blast, crackling like lightning.

It struck a warlock in the chest, causing him to convulse before he fell to the ground. A stream of green shot past her ear. She leaned back, conjuring a ball of red light between her fingers. She breathed slowly, focused. With a shout, she hurled it at the front line. It exploded into a wall of red, separating the witches of her coven from those of the Dark Ring.

Both sides exploded from the barrier. Some hit the hard dirt while others crashed into trees. Breathing fast, Morgan tried to cushion the blow of every one of her witches. Throwing protective spells with her right hand while conjuring another ball of red light with her left.

"Run!" she screamed at them, finally adding her right hand to the crackling sphere in her hands. The wall she had erected between the two sides started to fade, and she advanced, growing the ball of energy until it was one foot in diameter. She hurled it at the Dark Ring.

Several of Zachariah's disciples lifted their arms, creating a shield. The ball of energy crashed into them, sending them reeling but otherwise unharmed. Several others formed energy waves and launched them at Morgan. She jumped and spun, the whump, whump of the waves as they flew through the air growing louder as they passed by. The waves of energy missed her by mere inches; she could feel the heat radiating from each.

A tree exploded behind Morgan. Wood fragments descending around her as the tree began to fall. She landed on one knee. Her right hand rose above her to form a shield, her left hand steadying her kneeling position. The tree crashed into her shield, splitting into thousands of pieces.

She lifted her left hand and forced the splinters to rise before many had touched the ground. They rose like spears, aimed at the Dark Ring. With a shriek, she pushed her right hand forward in a palm strike.

Zachariah's disciples screamed as the hail of wood splinters raining down on them. Some of the horde put up shields just in time, while others fell, blood issuing from their gaping wounds.

Morgan stood, eyes fixed on the group. A blast of orange careened toward her head, but she deflected it with ease, like swatting away a fly. Another shot aimed for her legs, and she dive rolled, the spell causing an explosion of dust behind her. She began to advance. Her body crackled with red energy, her red, curly hair seeming to emit sparks of fire.

Several of the Dark Ring had regained their composures and stood with feet firmly planted. Almost without a thought, she pushed them aside with a wave of red, pinning them to the forest trees. Many tried to struggle, but others simply gasped from the impact and fainted.

There were still some thirty more members of Zachariah's group standing, arms raised and fingers emitting their own sparks of black.

Morgan stopped, dropping her hands but still radiating fire. "Where is he?"

They said nothing, remaining fixed in attack position.

She called again, this time with more determination. "Where is he?"

"Is it Zachariah you're looking for, or me?"

The voice came from behind a crowd of disciples, sinister and quiet, though cutting through the air like a knife. Morgan's mouth curled downward, and she shook her hands, blazing red electricity balling in her palms. She could smell him now. It was a burning smell of ash, faint but definitely present.

A man cut through the Dark Ring with green energy sparking at his fingertips. His eyes were slanted, and his nose crooked. His wavy hair was perfectly coiffed, falling down to his shoulders. He might have been handsome, if not for his black eyes. He smirked, drawing up his lips in a half smile.

"Seth."

"And who else?" He raised his hands and twirled exuberantly.

One of the disciples attempted to slash her with a cutting spell. Still, Morgan brought up her hand in a chop, slamming him against a nearby tree and knocking him unconscious. "You brought your dogs, I see."

His smile quivered, and then recovered. "I'm only here as a messenger."

"To what, kill me?" She let out a fake laugh, presenting more confidence than she felt.

"Well, we've tried… other options." He looked her up and down, causing her cheeks to burn. When he saw her face redden, he smiled wickedly.

Suddenly, her heart was beating very quickly. In a matter of mere moments, he had cut her down to a frightened girl. But she tossed her hair back, feigning the authority she did not feel.

"Kill her," he said, nonchalantly, and turned to leave.

Morgan drew her hands into an X above her head, and then slashed downward. All members of the Dark Ring were ejected from their spots, flying through the air in a blaze of dust. Two lines of red, still visible, cut a V in the ground with an area narrow enough for only one person: Seth.

He turned back to her with a cocked head, a smile still pasted on his lips. He tsked. "Don't lose your temper now."

She snorted, letting her hands fall to her sides. "I knew you missed me."

Seth shot a beam of black light at Morgan. She dodged, only to be met with another blast inches from her face. She leaped backward, slamming a hand to the ground and forcing red lightning to erupt from the earth.

He rose, sending a swirl of black below him to catapult him off the ground. Morgan jumped up forcefully, and side kicked him in the chest, sending him reeling. He recovered quickly, running to meet her, the smile still creeping on his lips.

Seth struck with a back fist. Morgan blocked, grabbed his arm, and pulled him toward her as she threw a knee. He dodged with a slice of black, leaving a gash on her leg. Undeterred, she locked his arm, forcing a grunt from him. His eyes bulged, but he made no further sound. Her hand snaked to the back of his neck, her free hand crackling as a ball of electricity mushroomed. Just as she struck, a ball of black collided with her own red one, sending both of them soaring in opposite directions.

She was blinded for a moment, the great bolt of light disappearing gradually from her eyes. The arm which had held him in a lock was broken in two places. Bone protruded from her elbow and through her forearm.

Taking a deep breath, she forced her red energy to course through her arm. The clacking of mending bones accompanied the pain of her bones retreating into her skin. The blood from her wounds crowded the repairs and then sealed the wounds. The tick of muscles knitting together in her knee continued for several moments before the injury was finally closed. The rest of the blood she burned off with a blaze of red light.

Seth was slowly rising to his feet as Morgan stood. A smirk of her own crossing her face. Seth's people were still either pinned to the ground, to trees or lying unconscious. All it would take was another strike at him, and he would be finished, Zachariah's militant army reduced to merely a few disciples.

She walked toward him, feeling the heat from her magic pressing through her body. She was completely ablaze. Flickering flames danced at the top of her head.

The smile had been wiped from Seth's face, and his perfectly set hair now hung down in streaks. He breathed heavily, and his shoulders crumpled slightly. But his eyes remained on Morgan's.

"What now, Seth? I'll kill you and send the rest of these miscreants back to their master."

He remained silent for what seemed like an eternity, and Morgan came to a stop only five feet from him.

Finally, she continued. "Nothing to say?" She snorted and let her blazing hands drop to her sides. "I thought you would be more of a challenge than that."

Though faint, she heard footsteps behind her, possibly from her sisters. She smirked. It was only a matter of time now before the rest of Zachariah's army was brought to dust. He would be too weak to come after them.

"Morgan!" It was Jayden. Despite herself, she looked over her shoulder to see him smiling at her, out of breath.

A deep, searing pain erupted in her stomach. She couldn't breathe. She couldn't move. Seth's grin returned as he plunged the dagger further into her gut, angling it upward, closer to her heart. Serrated edges dug into her flesh, making blood flow freely from the wound. She stood, shocked, staring at Seth as he forced the blade to its hilt.

He pulled it out with a ragged jerk, pulling a string of skin from her stomach. She dropped to her knees as she continued to stare into his eyes.

He hit the ground with a tight fist, sending green sparks flying toward the disciples and releasing them from their captivity. Those who had been knocked unconscious sprang to life and started to run, dragging wounded companions with them.

Morgan saw streaks of blue and yellow all around her, but she could do nothing but kneel, the gut-wrenching pain overtaking her senses. She blinked in shifts, each eyelid seeming to move of its own accord. She looked down at a hand that had been clenched to her stomach. It was stained with red—blood and magic.

THREE

The Binding

MORGAN DRIFTED IN AND OUT OF CONSCIOUSNESS. SHE could feel her body starting to give up. There was just so much blood; every inch of her seemed to be covered in it. She put a hand on her stomach to try to stem the flow, but she couldn't feel anything. She sank to the ground.

A figure was at her side, also dipping his hand into her stomach. The red contrasted dramatically with his white shirt. She fell in a stupor when she smiled. The blurred outline of a man fading in and out of her sight. She wasn't sure if he was moving or if her vision was cutting out. The bloody hand came up to her face and moved her chin back and forth rapidly.

Morgan blinked, trying to move her head away from the jostling. She was getting a headache, but the hand refused to let go of her chin. It began to lightly tap on her on the cheek, then suddenly with more force. A moaning sounded out of nowhere, like an ethereal presence. She couldn't find out where it came from, only that it wouldn't stop.

Slowly, she brought her blood-stained hand up to her

mouth, only to find that it was her making the noise. Nothing seemed to make sense. The world was moving slowly, and she could barely keep her eyes open.

"Wake up, wake up!"

The voice shouting in her ear sounded panicked, but she couldn't recognize the problem. Wake? Why? It seemed much easier to sleep.

"Jayden?" she asked wearily. She could only just see his face through the flashes of fading blue and yellow.

He was shaking her head again, his other hand grasped around her back. She let out another moan and attempted to sit up but was met with excruciating pain.

Suddenly, her mind fought back, and her vision cleared. She was lying on her back. Her knees at an odd angle behind her. Her spine was arched, contorted. Every movement brought pain, and it intensified gradually until it became a piercing roar.

Morgan cried out, lifting her head and shaking it slightly to clear her mind. Every bone ached. Every muscle cried out in agony. She couldn't move. She couldn't breathe. Morgan lifted both hands to her face and registered the blood for the first time. Panic rose with a lump in her throat, and immediately she couldn't breathe. What blood was left, she felt pounding in her ears. Her mind cried out with every movement, even the batting of an eyelash.

"Jayden?" Morgan said again, feeling herself start to tear up. She was hyperventilating. She could feel it, but she couldn't stop. Looking down, she felt her breath become even more rapid.

The knife Seth had used left a hole in her gut, a pool of red leaking from both sides. The blood shined in the light as she breathed, and the magic pooled around her sides, a stream of it rising up and dissipating in a cloud of steam.

She reached out desperately, doing her best to grab the magic outside of her body and force it back into her, to no avail. It kept seeping out. She willed herself to heal, but nothing happened. The wound remained open.

Morgan cried out in desperation, holding up her shaking hands to see the red power that normally crackled there. Nothing. She began tearing at her corset, forcing it open and revealing the white, baggy shirt underneath. The red stain continued to grow, making her wet and sticky.

She tried to rip the shirt open, but Jayden caught her hands. Morgan stared up at him. She screamed and tried to fight him, but Jayden held her weak arms back.

"Alaina, Brenna!" he was screaming. "Lie still," he said forcefully, pinning her hands to the ground. "Alaina, Brenna!" he shouted again. He cursed under his breath and called out to others.

The coven gathered around her. Morgan tried to swallow, but it caught in her throat. Her panic rose as the coven began to whisper among themselves.

"Do something." Jayden sounded urgent. It was apparent he was attempting to stay calm.

Fabian knelt beside them both, sending waves of purple into her stomach with shaking hands. Nothing. Elsie stepped by him and added her magic to his, pouring in a crackle of orange sparks. Still nothing.

One witch after another attempted to close the wound, but none succeeded.

Jayden stood, running his hands through his hair and smearing her blood onto his scalp. He turned away for a moment, his head falling into his hands. Finally, he looked back. "I'm out of ideas," he admitted, exasperated. "What would you have me do?"

"That weapon used," Fabian said calmly, "do you

know what it looked like?" No one said a word, glancing among themselves only to shake their heads quickly.

Morgan tried to recall, but events were getting fuzzy. It had a symbol, an ancient one, but she couldn't remember the details. Every time she pressed her mind for information, a blazing headache prevented her from getting too far.

She fought the pain long enough to reach out to him. He grasped her hand immediately.

"I don't know what he's done to me," she said. Blood started to creep down the side of Morgan's mouth, and her eyes widened slightly. She choked it down and continued, "It's likely some sort of spell. Seth... struck me with a dagger. It must have had a spell etched on it or something. I haven't seen it before." She took a moment to regulate her breath, which was becoming choppy with the blood entering her lungs.

"I can only think of one thing. A spell. I have to bond with someone before it's too late."

"I'll do it."

"Jayden, you don't know the risks. You're mortal. I don't know what this could do to you."

"I don't care."

"Jayden—"

"Please." It was a whisper, a faint noise that started in his throat and moved down through his gut. She saw his desperation, and this time didn't divert her eyes when he stared down at her.

"Go get Alaina. She'll know what to do."

FOUR

The Price

JAYDEN SPRINTED AWAY, BUT MORGAN COULD ONLY KEEP AN eye on him for a moment before her head became too cumbersome. It sank with a thud. She started to cough, and red sprayed in a lethal mist above her head. The blood particles dusted her face, and she closed her eyes against the sting.

"Any minute now," someone was saying to her. It was getting harder to concentrate. The adrenaline rush from the initial wound had long since faded, and she lay in agony on the ground, moments from passing out.

The thud of footsteps sounded around her, but her dizzy mind didn't even attempt to recognize the owners. Instead, she lay back, trying her best to ignore the pain. Her breath was stained with blood, and she tried desperately not to cough.

"I'm here," Alaina's voice said in a faint whisper.

Morgan reached a hand out to grasp her sister. "The Alchemy," she said quietly. "The Binding spell."

Alaina swallowed hard but said nothing else. Morgan opened her eyes only enough to see Alaina nod, moving her hands to cover both Morgan and Jayden. She began to chant in soft, soothing words that sounded like riddles. Yellow light gently floated down to the cut in her stomach, and she could feel her breathing beginning to ease.

After a few moments, Brenna joined Alaina, laying an arm on Alaina's shoulder and chanting in the same, soothing voice. The blue light came in flashes among the yellow. Both of them began to sway as they closed their eyes and spoke the words in unison.

There was a gurgling noise and then a cough. Morgan opened her eyes and turned to her left to see Jayden coughing, spitting up blood. Alarmed, she laid a hand on his, soothing him. He returned the favor.

It was getting easier to breathe. Morgan drew in a healthy gasp and let out a sigh of relief. Through the corner of her eye, she could see her own wound healing slowly. The muscles were knitting together. Strings of flesh seemed to wake and knot themselves tidily, forming a smooth surface.

The last bit of her red magic that had been seeping through the hole in her gut ceased to flow. Instead, it began moving through the rest of her body. Red sparks snaked their way along her left arm and into Jayden. She gasped at the sensation, taken aback at the friction it caused in her body.

Jayden grimaced. As the spell continued, his grip increased, and it was all Morgan could do to stop from making a sound. She fought through the pain as the rest of her body began to heal.

He coughed again, still expelling blood, but it was paler. Every breath seemed to come at a high cost, so there were moments when he refrained from breathing altogether. He made an audible groan, his back arching.

"Hold on," Morgan whispered. She squeezed back as

hard as she could, feeling their connection inspire sparks of red. She was drifting in and out of consciousness. Her only reality was the hand she had grasped with Jayden's. As though it were her lifeline.

Jayden glanced over at her and gave her a forced smile. "Don't... worry," he said through knotted words.

Her body seemed lighter, full of energy. But there was something wrong. It was mainly as if something else was oozing from her body. Morgan gasped, her eyes opening wide. Suddenly, the warmth that had sustained her through the healing process became a stab of agony. Starting from the bottom of her feet and slowly rising to the top of her head. White light was drawing away from her.

Morgan held her breath and stared straight ahead, fearful of looking anywhere else. The white light reached her stomach, stopped for a moment, then continued to rise at an increased speed.

She felt a knot in her throat and tried to swallow it, but it didn't work. With an exhale, she saw a small ball of white light leave through her breath. Morgan watched it float into the sky, her whole body tense. It drifted above her for a moment, maybe more. She couldn't be sure. Just like a flame, it grew smaller with time, finally disappearing with a puff of smoke.

This was it. She had sacrificed her immortality.

All went black.

FIVE

Attacks

SHE COULD DETECT VOICES, BUT THEY WERE FAR AWAY. Whispers sounded in dark corners, and she couldn't muster the strength to open her eyes. It felt as though her body had been trampled, and the pain in her abdomen still potent. Instead of chancing additional discomfort, she stayed still, listening intently.

"Are you sure?"

"Of course, I am." It was Jayden. "I heard them muttering it as they left. They thought they killed her. According to Zachariah, we all are as good as dead."

"Ridiculous," Alaina spoke this time. "He must have known that the rest of us would have been able to finish him off. It is just his overconfidence that fuels those rumors."

"But did you see her?" Another witch was speaking now, though Morgan could not determine who. "Before she showed up, we were falling back. Even without Seth working against us, the rest of the Dark Ring was pushing us back. Gwen is dead because of it. They had us pinned down, with only a few of us left. If she hadn't come and ended it, we'd all be dead now."

Alaina scoffed. "Do you honestly believe that we will be nothing without her? Surely we can take Zachariah all at once if we stick together. Just Brenna and I can take that horde if it comes to it. Look at her." She paused for a moment, and Morgan felt all eyes on her. "She's been unconscious for two days and doesn't show any signs of recovering quickly. This has to be done without her."

"No." Brenna finally spoke up, and Morgan felt a shift in the air. "Alaina, you've always been a hothead. Morgan is the key to taking down Zachariah, and we must wait until she recovers before we proceed."

"Just because you are the oldest does not mean that you have all the knowledge about this. Don't be an idiot. We have to face all sides, and Morgan is not the end-all-be-all of this operation."

Morgan felt a wave of anger that didn't come from herself. It pierced her mind, and she flinched involuntarily. This rage felt new, yet old, as though it had festered for some time, but she had never experienced it before.

A fist banged down on the table, and she could feel her red energy radiating from the closed fist. "Seth has said that Morgan is his greatest threat. Even if you don't believe that he does. She has greater powers than most of you in this room combined." Morgan could feel Jayden's teeth grind together.

"If you had any sense, you would keep your mouth shut, mortal," Alaina hissed.

Jayden never said a word, but Morgan could feel the power flushing through his body and into his hands. Though imperceptible to many, she felt the sparks in his fingertips—her own magic flowing through his body. The rage she felt nearly choked her. She couldn't help but gasp for breath, the magic within her flaring.

"Morgan." Jayden was by her side, stroking her hair as she fought to open her eyes. Suddenly, the rage that had filled her body was gone. She gingerly raised a hand to his chest, calming the storm within.

"Careful, Jayden," she said with a faint smile.

He put his arm around her and forced her upward. She gave a cry of pain, but he continued to pull. Finally, she sat, allowing her head to fall forward.

She could feel Brenna close to her now, and she put a hand on Morgan's knee. "Good to see you awake."

Morgan's eyes opened to slits, and she snickered under her breath. "Yeah, I'll bet you are excited to see me awake."

"Morgan." Alaina was standing some five feet away, wringing her hands. Though she stood with an air of confidence, Morgan knew that Alaina feared her slightly.

"Everyone stop saying my name," Morgan said with another laugh. "I get tired of it enough hearing it in my own head to be hearing it from the lot of you for the next few hours." She tried to sink back against the wall behind her, but Jayden stopped her.

"Oh, no, you don't. You may be woozy, but I think falling through the wall of a tent might just wake you up a bit too much."

"Sassy," she said under her breath and straightened her back instead. "What is this chatter all about? Just because I was nearly dead doesn't mean I should be out of the loop. Tell me what's happened." She tried to stand, but her legs gave way. She reached out to Jayden for support, and he grabbed her hand, steadying her. "What, Jayden, no sweeping me into your arms."

"You do well enough on your own. I've never coddled you in the past, and I'm not about to do it now." He smirked at her, and she responded by sticking her tongue out. He maneuvered her over to the table and dragged out a chair for her.

Before she could sit down, the chair flew from beneath her, and she fell flat on her backside, crying out indignantly. "And what was that for?"

"Sorry, sorry," Jayden said nonchalantly. He looked at his fingers, and red sparks erupted from them, nearly singing his brows. "Still getting used to this stuff. How do you control this, anyway?"

"You'll learn, young one," Morgan said, grabbing his hand and standing. "For now, though, I think I'll have someone else get my chair."

She smiled almost sleepily as she waltzed jaggedly to the chair. She made a point of dragging it roughly across the ground before depositing it before the table and falling into it. She winced slightly from the pain, and she noticed he had, as well.

"For heaven's sake, man," she said, looking Jayden up and down as he sat down next to her. "Get a new shirt."

"Obviously, something happened—" Brenna began.

"Well, obviously." Morgan raised her right hand and tugged on her magic. Jayden's arm rose, too. She raised an eyebrow. "What's the matter? Did Alaina not read the inscription correctly? I wouldn't be surprised."

Yellow light singed at the ends of Alaina's fingertips, and her eyes blazed, but Morgan waved her off with a smile.

"Of course, we didn't know the effects of the spell until recently," Brenna said, running a finger along with the pages of The Alchemy. "We might be able to recreate it, given enough time. There are several ingredients necessary, of course, but we don't have them all with us. Bloodroot, for one; we used the last of it on you two days ago. If you hadn't gone off by yourself—"

Morgan lifted a hand. "Let's not even discuss that right now. I'm not quite over it myself."

"I'll set out for it—" Brenna tried to continue.

"There isn't time, and you have not finished your recovery cycle. You were supposed to rest also. You are not nearly up to the capacity of completing this binding spell in your condition. That's probably why it backfired in the first place. If you haven't gathered enough strength by the time Zachariah strikes again, we'll surely be outnumbered, and maybe even dead." Morgan felt a pang of worry and shot Jayden a look of incredulity.

Brenna only nodded once, her eyes slightly downcast.

"And Alaina, you must get some rest as well. Your body was in a coma. If you are not strong enough, it's only a matter of time before you become too weak."

Alaina's eyes flared again. "I will not. You need me."

"Good heavens, girl. You're nearly 534, and it's like putting a toddler down for a nap! Yes, I know, you're body is only 28. Just trust me." She put her hand out to grasp her sister's. "It'll only be a few days until you've rested enough, and I'd rather do without you for a few days than find you dead at the hand of Zachariah." Morgan shook her sister's hand, forcing Alaina to stare into her eyes. "Hey. I'm doing this for you."

She smiled, but Alaina only nodded.

Morgan bid them farewell as they entered the Old 35 Highway and headed off down the old dirt road. She continued to wave as the car disappeared over the horizon. Brenna had said that both Noah and Caleb would be at the site, waiting for them. The three sisters had been separated for years, with only a brief reuniting. Morgan still didn't know so much about her siblings.

Morgan felt an ache in her gut where she had been stabbed, but she shook it off. Alaina and Brenna had retreated into their regeneration states, and Morgan alone stood as the head of the coven. She had returned to a leather corset and pants. Her hair was tied in a knot on her head as a sort of beacon to her mind to concentrate. Sometimes, they seemed like the only things holding her together.

She studied the map in front of her. It was new, drawn only a year or so ago. The coven had been traveling so much in the last few years that a new map needed to be drawn almost semi-annually. They should have a party, Morgan thought with a breathy snort.

"Still poring over the maps, I see." Jayden had been around a lot lately, partly because she could not physically be away from him for long. The binding spell made her feel nauseous every time she drifted too far. Though this time, he had taken her by surprise.

"Don't scare me like that," she said half-jokingly, but she pressed a hand to her stomach to add pressure to the wound.

"I haven't seen your hair like that in a long time." He reached out his hand to run a finger through a curl.

She smacked his hand away in irritation. "Don't do that."

"And why not?"

"Because I told you not to, pinhead."

"I'll do what I very well like," he said, feigning an attack from the front but batting her lightly in the bun from behind.

Annoyed, she flicked a finger, sending his heel rising into the air, his head some feet above the ground.

Before she could turn back to her maps, however, she felt her own heel jerking toward the sky, and she lay upside down, swinging in the air, blood rushing to her face. Her shock was broken by the guffawing laughter coming, not two feet away from her.

"Ah, now you've done it, you fool. Got us into this mess." Jayden pushed her side playfully, causing her to spin. "I could have quite a lot of fun with this."

Exasperated, she flicked her finger again, forcing both of them to fall to the ground. Her bushy red hair flying free from her clasp and covering her face as her cheeks brightened. Standing, she spat out a large chunk of her hair and glared at him playfully. "I'll show you who's the fool," she said, mischievously punching him on the shoulder. He only half defended himself as he continued to laugh.

A loud bang and a scream echoed from across the forest. Morgan turned, first to the forest, and then to Jayden. They stared at each other for a moment before both ran as fast as they could toward the sound.

Trees whipped by them, and Morgan found herself falling slightly short of Jayden's stride. Ignoring the pain the running caused, she sprinted onward. Leaves and brambles whipped at her face, but she could hardly feel the cuts, her body filled with adrenaline not entirely her own.

Jayden stopped ahead and held up a hand behind him. She slowed, hunching down and hiding among the trees. Someone was running away in a hurry, his black cloak trailing behind him. Just ahead, there was a mound on the ground with sandy blond hair cut short: James.

Morgan tried to send a blast from her magic reserves, but the spell did not make it far, exploding in the air. Just mere feet away from the intruder. Morgan shook her hands and tried again with the same result. She looked at Jayden, suddenly worried.

"Let him go," he said, grabbing her hand and pulling her over to James.

James lay in a pool of orange and gray matter, his magic seeping from his eyes and mouth. A large bruise covered his neck. His eyes remained open. He was dead.

Morgan's first instinct was to strike, and she ran after the fleeing man no longer in view, but an excruciating pain in her head made her stop and fall. She screamed in desperation, fire burning at the tips of her fingers. She turned back to Jayden in a rage.

He knelt next to James, obviously feeling the same emotions that she did but not moving from his spot. His hand gently closed the lids of the fallen witch as he whispered something softly. His hand was engulfed with red fire, which lashed out every few seconds like a heartbeat. James looked broken but otherwise peaceful. Jayden lifted a crystal from around James' neck. As soon as the crystal left his skin, James burst into a cloud of orange dust. Jayden continued to kneel, clenching the crystal in his hands.

Suddenly, she was overcome by grief, something Morgan had trained herself to overcome quickly. She felt tears sting her eyes, which she wiped away angrily.

"Come on," Jayden said, standing and walking briskly back to camp.

She still felt the grief dig at her insides and knew that it must come from Jayden. He remained stone-faced as he headed off. She was impressed despite herself.

He stopped short just a few minutes after setting off and wheeled on her. "There is no need to feel impressed. A man just died, Morgan." He gestured toward the grove of trees they had just left, the rope from the crystal swinging wildly. "Can you think of nothing but the chase?" He stepped closer to her. "He's dead."

Though several hundred years his senior, she looked

down, ashamed. "I'm sorry." She didn't think of an excuse. There wasn't one. She felt a stinging pain in her palm, and she glanced up to see Jayden's hand, the one clutching the crystal, dripping blood. She said nothing.

Jayden turned back again and marched. They did not speak as they went. The emotions and thoughts in their heads doing all the conversing for them.

Just before they reached camp, Jayden stopped her. "Sibyl was sweet on him. Better tell her." He opened his hand and dumped the emerald jewel into her waiting hand.

Five more strikes left another five dead, and all were grieved. Of those five, an additional three were lost from Zachariah's Dark Ring. They lay in crumpled heaps not far from her own people. She was forced to take Jayden with her now, but she battled back her natural tendencies to fight before tending to the dead.

It was the evening of the third day when Jayden finally pulled her aside to talk. "Those witches were young, and you're not, but I knew them individually. I'm sorry for pushing you aside. That wasn't fair."

She felt an encircling compassion she hadn't for years, and she almost reached her hand up to his face but stopped. Connected as they were, though, Jayden closed his eyes slowly and gently smiled.

"I know I'm not used to it, but we can do this, do you hear me? I know you've got it in you."

"I can't use my magic like I used to. You're stopping me from accessing it all at once." She let out a sigh of desperation and ran her fingers through her hair. "I just don't know how this is going to work."

"Then I guess we'd better get practicing."

SIX

Unison

"WHAT YOU WANT TO DO IS POINT YOUR HAND TOWARD THE tree stump. Imagine lifting it with your mind." Morgan stood next to Jayden, lifting her hands without using magic to demonstrate the motion. "See? Now, I'm going to do it here, and I'll give you an easier one later. Maybe lift a block of wood you cut this morning."

Jayden was rooted on the stump in the ground, breathing slowly and slightly shakily. He nodded a few times, loosening his body by jumping.

Morgan smiled. "No need to worry. It only takes practice. You can get the hang of it." He nodded again. Chuckling under her breath, she extended her hand and firmly pulled the stump from the ground. Roots clung desperately to the soil, but she continued to apply force. At last, she had it hovering in the air, dust, and mud occasionally dripping from the tree stump.

"Now, not so bad, right? Did you feel how my magic moved as I pulled it out of the ground? All it takes is a constant motion to pull it out. Now you try." She pointed to a block of wood on the ground several feet in front of them. "I know you know how it works since you're connected to me. So, just do what I did."

Morgan let Jayden take the lead, his hand making the motion instead of hers. As he pulled up, Morgan's arm lifted with his, their magic connecting their limbs. The block of wood started to shake on the ground. Its wobbling intensified as his brows furrowed.

"Take it easy," Morgan urged quietly. "Don't force it too much. Just let it work for you."

The block of wood started to tremble faster, harder. Jayden's eyebrows were now embedded in his eyelashes, and his teeth gritted. Morgan felt the magic pulling quickly, a little too quickly. Before she had a chance to slow him down, the block of wood exploded. She held up a hand to block the shower of splinters headed for them.

Someone yelled in the distance, "Hey! Watch it! I just got the splinters out of my backside after the last time you tried this!"

Morgan turned to Jayden with an exaggerated sigh. "See, this is what happens when you try too hard. You're going to bite your own tongue out, and Tom will be cleaning out his butt for a month."

"Well, it might be easier if you shut your mouth for a moment. That way, I could concentrate without hearing a yap in my ear every time something goes wrong." He shot her an effortless smile.

"So snippy, young one."

"And always with the 'young one.' You know, most women aren't too fond of discussing their ages, but you can't seem to get enough of it, you old lady."

She batted him lightly on the shoulder.

He swatted her back with a glowing red hand, sending both of them flying in opposite directions.

"All right, it's time to conjure something." She rubbed

her shoulder, where she had impacted the ground. You suck at this, she thought.

"Yes, I do," Jayden said matter-of-factly as he walked up to her.

"Stop," she said in a whine.

"What? I can't help it if you're constantly blathering on in your mind. It's like a constant stream of inner thought. I can't differentiate my own thoughts from yours now. I'm starting to wonder if I honestly am that handsome." I'm beginning to wonder if I really am that handsome." He flashed a knowing smile then looked back at the exploded piece of wood.

Morgan flushed slightly. She looked up at him through a furrowed brow, her mouth firming into a bemused slit.

Jayden didn't look back, only shaking his shoulders teasingly.

"You're about this close to getting a wallop," she warned, holding up her fingers a fraction of an inch apart.

"I'll bet you'd like that, wouldn't you?"

"Okay, you have to stop," she said, trying not to laugh. She turned, both of them facing the same direction. "So, let's do something simple like sparking a fire in your hand." Morgan held out her right hand, crunched it into a fist, and then spread her fingers with a jolt. A small flame ignited in her palm.

Jayden stared at it for quite some time before nodding slowly, forming a fist, and then splaying his fingers. A tiny spark ignited then fell passively to the forest floor.

"Wow," Morgan said, raising her eyebrows and staring at the spot where the spark landed. "Just... wow. I really thought you'd have the hang of this one since you've been causing explosions all morning."

Jayden looked down, too, letting out an exasperated

sigh. "Maybe we've been going about this in the wrong way."

"Well, since the most direct route hasn't worked, I'd say you're right."

Jayden turned to her, not saying anything for a moment, then waved a hand away from the area where they were practicing. "Come on."

They walked back to camp in silence. Though they were always connected, Morgan couldn't access his feelings. He was a complete blank. As they reached the clearing with the tents, Jayden made a detour and headed for the woodpile. Bewildered, Morgan followed.

Jayden had set up a small logging area where some 30 or more logs were collected. Since he had no magic of his own, other witches had contributed to the pile daily. Most of his day was spent here, splitting wood and studying herbs. Hanging from a tree branch were several strips of leather. He pulled two from their perch and summoned her to come nearer. She obliged.

"Do you remember when I was ten years old? You saved me from that fire that Zachariah had started?" Moving closer to her, he tied one strap of leather around both of their legs at the thigh. "I often wondered how you ended up finding me there." The other piece of leather, he tied around their calves. "You seemed to be at the right place at the right time, and everyone else in the village was dead." He stood straight and stared at her. "How did you know?"

"Come on, Jayden," she said, looking down at the leather straps and smiling. "This is ridiculous."

"Don't worry about the straps and answer the question. How did you know I was there?"

"I don't know," Morgan said, still not looking at him.

"You didn't have magic. Your sister did. Maybe that's how we were able to find you."

"But my sister was dead long before you and your sisters showed up. How did you know?"

Morgan looked up at him. His usually jovial expression had changed into something more sullen. He really was concerned about the answer. "I can't really explain it. We saw the fire and went to help, I guess. We didn't have a lot of witches in the coven at that point, and it was shortly after Zachariah had gone after us the last time. I guess I just figured that there must have been some reason that Zachariah wanted to burn your town."

Jayden dropped his gaze and gave a breathy snort. "Yes, I suppose."

They stood in silence for a moment, each staring at the ground. Even though they had known each other for years, they had barely spoken in more than jest. It really was incredible how they could spend so much time together and never really know who the other was.

Morgan broke the silence with the clearing of her throat. "So, what have you got in mind with this?"

"Well, since we can't be apart with the magic, we might as well try to stay together physically."

She groaned. "You know I detest this sort of thing."

"I know," he said with a wicked smile. "That's why I'm making you do it. If we stay together like this, we might start thinking the same thing, not just thinking the same way."

Morgan cocked her head quizzically but decided to let the confusion slide. "All right, then, left or right foot first?"

"Let's start off on the right foot. Hi, I'm Jayden." He stuck his hand out to her with a generous cheesy grin on his face.

"Oh, yeah," she said between deep breaths. "This is

going to be fun." She moved to take a step forward with her left leg, but got caught in the momentum and tumbled over sideways, taking him with her. They fell with a thud on the ground, him on top of her.

They stared at each other for a moment before she pushed him off. "Nope, nope, nope," she said, trying to get back to her feet but finding it difficult as he was pulling in the opposite direction.

"You're making this difficult."

"I'm making this difficult? What about you, you dunce? You're a great hulking tub of man, and you won't move a muscle." She sank back down to the ground, and they lay side by side for a few moments, both breathing rapidly. "This was stupid."

"You're stupid."

She back fisted him lightly in the chest. "You keep making that joke, but I don't think it's as funny as you think it is."

"Fine, all right. I see your point." He scrambled to his feet, dragging her with him.

"Wow, this leather is strong," she said, tugging at it. "What did you do to it?"

"Maybe you're just weak." He flashed a winning smile and untied the straps, moving them to their waists—a difficult task, being as how he was about a foot taller than she. After a moment of struggling, he simply tied a loop around each of their waists and connected them with a knot.

"You know, you could magically fuse them together," she pointed out. He made to move his hand toward the leather strap when Morgan stopped him. "On second thought, I'd better do it." She pointed a finger at the knot and forced the leather to weave itself together.

"Do you want lunch?"

"I by no means think this is the moment to think about—"

"I'm starving. Let's grab something to eat." Without much warning, he started to walk toward a table stocked with fruits, vegetables, and jerky. Grabbing some of each, he hoisted them into Morgan's arms. Soon, she was laden down with food. He pulled a blanket from beside a tent and sloppily wrapped the food in it. An apple slipped free, but Morgan seized it before it hit the ground.

"There's a perfectly good table right here," she told him. "I don't see the point of wrapping up food to take it somewhere else."

"I know you wouldn't." He said nothing else, just glanced at her with a grin.

He led her more than a mile from the camp, strolling as his giant stride often overtook hers. They climbed a small hill and sat among the trees on a bit of meadow grass. Whippoorwills and nightingales sang in the trees, but all else was quiet. It was growing dark, but Jayden laid the blanket out and sat down, taking her hand and pulling her down with him.

"I don't see the point of this."

"Tell me about you."

Morgan raised her eyebrows at him but looked away when he continued to stare. "Okay, well, I grew up some centuries ago—and you're not going to find out the exact date; a woman enjoys her mysteries—and I met you, and here we are now."

Jayden took a bite of an apple before letting out an exasperated sigh. "Maybe I'll go first. When I was a boy, I constantly daydreamed about going on an adventure. I saw the clouds and imagined myself floating by with them. I imagined I would have a horse and travel the countryside. I used to think that slaying dragons and rescuing fair maidens would make my family proud. I'd mount the heads of the dragons on the mantle and graciously drop off the maidens at some institution or other, always waiting for the next adventure."

"That's ridiculous," Morgan said, lying on her back. "There are no such things as dragons."

Jayden shrugged. "Perhaps not." He laughed lightly then lay down next to her. "Of course, as I got older, I realized the futility of my dream. No mantle in the whole country could fit the head of a dragon." He took another bite of the apple.

Morgan laughed.

"You see that bird up there?" The bird was red with a golden breast. It seemed to be floating in midair, carrying a worm in its mouth.

"Yes."

"Do you think it's feeding its young, or just enjoying its time in the sky?"

Morgan was silent, staring at it as it continued to hover.

"I think it's probably feeding its young. Things in this world like to help others, for the most part. Wouldn't you agree?" He turned his head to face her, taking another bite out of the apple.

"I don't know about that."

"I do." He looked back at the bird, the fading sun making its golden feathers glisten. "It's not impossible to see. I think there's a little good in everyone. Some make it hard to love, but there's always that glimmer of hope."

This time, she turned. "Is that why you've been so cross with me lately? I haven't had the opportunity to spend with other people?"

"Cross? Nah." He was silent for another moment before speaking again. "I do think that you expect a little too much of yourself, though. Sometimes, I think you get so lost in fighting someone or something else that you cannot stop for a moment to realize that you are exactly where you need to be."

"And where is that?"

"Living for now, not for the past."

The sun's last rays gleamed gloriously through the trees, leaving behind spots of golden light on the trees on the secluded side of the meadow. Clouds of red and orange floated gently overhead, the lightest touches of dark blue starting to emerge above them.

They remained silent, still staring up at the sky. Morgan grabbed for some raspberries and popped them in her mouth, chewing slowly. "I lied to you before."

"I know."

She went quiet at that. Of course, he knew. He was in her head. He could feel what she felt about the night she found him.

"Tell me about Kian."

"I don't want to talk about him."

"I know, but tell me anyway."

Morgan realized she was holding her breath and released it slowly. It took her some time, but she finally spoke. "He was a mortal, like you. He didn't have any magic. I found him riding through the countryside, off on some adventure or another. He was quiet, but he stopped to help me pick apples. He had that black hair, kind of messy. His smile was as white as a cloud."

She took another few breaths and swallowed hard. "I would only see him when I could break away from camp. He would come with me for walks, taking his time. He was never in a rush to get anywhere. He was my secret. I don't think I ever laughed so much as I did when I was with him."

"Is that why you saved me?"

Morgan quickly blinked the tears away. "No. No, I rescued you because you were on your own and only a child. I rescued you because you were special."

Jayden continued to breathe deeply, still not making eye contact with her, as if he knew it would make her uncomfortable. "Go on. About Kian."

"There's really not much more to tell," Morgan said, finally sitting up. She turned away from him to wipe tears from her eyes.

She felt a wave of compassion for herself and turned to see Jayden still lying down, staring at her, his hand coming down to rest on her back. "Morgan," he said in a whisper.

She bowed her head, her chest throbbing. Finally, she raised her eyes to the sky again. "He was only 27 when Zachariah killed him. He was so young. I don't know how he found out about us. He made me watch—" She stopped, her throat suddenly choked. It took several minutes of quiet sobs before she could speak again. "Zachariah made me watch as he slit his throat. He could have destroyed him with a thought, but instead, he slit his throat."

Morgan put her head in her hands, trying to get her sobs under control, but the tears flowed freely. "I'm sorry," she said once she caught her breath.

"It's all right," he said, gently rubbing her back.

He sat up slowly and turned her face toward his. She still had tears on her cheeks, and she didn't move, but her eyes found his. Gently, he stroked her chin and used his thumb to wipe away the tears. He was getting closer, but still, she didn't move. He glanced down at her lips occasionally, and she didn't pull back.

Slowly, almost imperceptibly, he pulled her closer to him, his lips hovering over hers. She could feel his breath on her face. A sudden wave of passion swept over her, and she let him run his fingers through her hair as she closed her eyes and their lips met.

Suddenly, she jerked back to reality and blasted her way through the leather, standing up fast. "No! I can't do this again." Her tears came even quicker, and she swiped them away angrily. Morgan turned away from him in agitation, her hands falling to her hips. "I need to get out of here."

Jayden exhaled in frustration. "Morgan, this has to work, at least for now. You and I are bound together. We hear each other's thoughts; we feel the same emotions. The best way to go about this is to get closer to each other. I can understand you better, and you can lean on me. It won't be like with Kian. I promise."

He stood up behind her and tried to put his arm around her waist, but she spun on him angrily and pushed him hard. "You don't know what it's like. How could you? You've never had someone so close to you, a best friend and confidant in the most desperate of times. You only care to get your fix."

She didn't mean it, but she stood her ground, glaring up at him.

"How can you even say that?" He was getting frustrated now. He was lashing out with his arms, sending sparks flying from his fingertips. "You lied to me, you said so yourself. You know as well as I do that the day we met, there was something else that drew you to me. Not that I was a boy of ten. Not that I was the brother of a witch.

"I was hidden in the house, which was on fire when you found me. How else could you have known? How else could you have seen me? There is no other explanation, is there?"

Morgan looked up at him, and the sound of the birds suddenly seemed deafening. "I don't know what it was,

Jayden. It's certainly too old an idea to bring up now." She closed her eyes, turning her gaze to the ground when she opened them again. She felt old for the first time in a long time. Tired. She knew he was right, but she dare not imagine herself with him. There were so many reasons not to.

"The only way to get through this," he said in a whisper, "is to trust and rely on each other. If you at least try to get close to me, it'll make an impact when the time comes. I've seen it with others in the coven. When they love each other, they become, I don't know…stronger."

"Love?" Morgan questioned, raising her head. "Love? Jayden, you may be a good match for me, but that doesn't mean that we are meant to fall in love."

Jayden opened his mouth to speak, and then closed it, shaking his head. His eyelids shut slowly, and then dug into his flesh. After a moment, he opened them again. "I am in love with you," he said breathlessly.

Morgan's heart dropped. She'd known he was, but somehow, hearing it out loud seemed final, decisive. She bit the inside of her cheek, her eyes returning to the ground.

"Love," she said, just as breathlessly, "is a weakness. Alaina was in love with a witch once. Damon Foster was his name. Perhaps she did gain some power when fighting with him, but we later learned he was working with Zachariah. When he died next to her, she also died. Sometimes, she seems a husk of what she used to be, though she's had over three centuries to heal. Some bits remain."

"You're wrong, and I'll be the one to show you why."

They strode in silence back to the camp. It was well past dark when they eventually made it back. Most were still gathered around the fire.

"Anything to report?" Morgan asked.

"Nothing so far," Sibyl replied, her eyes never moving from the flames.

"Good. I'm heading off to bed. Set Fabian as the watch for the night. If he has trouble staying awake, find someone else to relieve him." She said nothing else, walking resolutely toward her tent. When she felt an aching of pain in her head, she shifted to see Jayden still by the fire. "Come on, then," she said.

They proceeded to walk in silence until they had arrived at her tent. "I'll need you close by tonight. I've not gotten a decent amount of sleep for the past week, and I can't be waking up with a headache when you roll over."

Jayden nodded and set up a bedroll at the base of her bed. "Goodnight."

He was melancholy, perhaps rightfully so. Still, she remained obstinate, being careful not to fall into the same patterns as before. It was too easy to feel resentful toward him, too easy to feel dejected.

She remained awake for an hour or so, never hearing Jayden's own heavy breathing indicating his sleep.

△▽△

MORGAN POURED through The Alchemy to find something that might protect them from the seemingly never-ceasing onslaught of attacks on individual witches. Luckily, they hadn't had any recent deaths. The coven had stayed in a relatively close group ever since the last few attacks.

"This one might work," Morgan said under her breath.

"What was that?"

It was rather annoying that Jayden had to stay no further than five feet away from her at all times. Still, intense breath and meditation exercises seemed to give her some solace. Breathing deeply to suffocate her aggravation, she replied, "A spell. It might just be what we're looking for."

Jayden leaned closely, and she could smell his hair as it drifted near her cheek. She felt a wave of attraction. Realizing it was her own; she cleared her throat and stepped away slightly.

He brandished a smile at her but said nothing. They both knew what the other was thinking. He looked down at the book, the smile still on his lips. "Yes, I see how that could work." Though he was no witch, he certainly was a scholar. He had spent so much time pouring over books, he knew more than she did. "Of course, you're going to need more than one witch to help you out with this one."

"I figured… you could help me."

He turned to her in an exaggerated surprise. "Me?"

"Well," she said, turning back to the book, "you do have half of my magic, so it only makes sense that you would help out. If you work through me, we can do it. Besides, you've been improving over the last few days." She gave him a smile.

It was rare for her to smile at him now. There seemed too much baggage for there to be a clean connection with them anymore.

"Right on," he said, giving her a melodramatic pat on the back. "So be it."

They headed to the edge of the forest and lifted their hands. Using smooth movements, they simulated the motion of water. Since they had been mentally connected for close to two weeks, it was becoming easier for them to follow each other's actions.

Red energy flowed from their fingertips, coming in a gentle stream. She stood closer to him as they practiced the movements. They were nearly in sync.

"Now, stand behind me."

Jayden moved behind her, both arms stretching in front of them. They continued the movements. Their arms drifting back and forth. She could feel him bending his body with hers. The movement became more syncopated, turning almost into a dance. Closing her eyes, she envisioned their movements in a waltz, his arms close to hers. Spinning, sweeping.

It took several minutes for them to complete the spell, and a shimmering wall of red sparkled in the light of the noon day sun. They lowered their hands in unison. Jayden's coming to rest at his sides.

Morgan could feel the cool breathing in his chest. She had drifted closer to him. With a sigh, she lightly rested her head on his chest.

"I think we can do this," he said quietly. "You and I."

SEVEN

Awake

IT WAS ALMOST WITH A SENSE OF RELIEF THAT MORGAN realized Brenna was finally reaching the edge of the camp. She woke up to see Jayden lying on the floor in his bedroll, his head turned to the side with his mouth slightly open.

He looked disheveled. He hadn't had a proper bath in the last few weeks since they were tethered together. Of course, she hadn't either.

She blinked rapidly, forcing his eyelids to flutter open. He rubbed his face hard with both hands. "Do you really have to do that?" he asked through his hands.

"Well, seeing as I can't go anywhere without you now, yes." She pushed at him playfully. "Come on. I haven't had a bath for a few weeks, and I reek. So do you. Grab some soap and let's head down to the river."

He peeked through his hands at her, looking shocked. "I'm not letting you see my... lower regions."

Morgan rolled her eyes. "And I'm not letting you see mine, either. Think of it as a swim. Take your underthings.

Sibyl was still awake and sitting next to the fire, poking

at the cinders. "Up so soon?" She glanced at both of them before returning her gaze to the flames.

"Jayden and I are headed for a swim. The barriers should be good enough to hold for quite some time, so there shouldn't be a problem. Is there anything else I can do to make your life easier?"

"Nope," Sibyl said, standing to stretch. "I think I'm going to find someone to relieve Laurie at the border, and then hit the sack."

"I don't know what I would do without you." Morgan grinned, and Sibyl smiled back, still stretching.

Morgan and Jayden headed out toward the river, smiling and chuckling at jokes the other told. As soon as they came to the river, they stripped down to their underclothes. Jayden dove into the water with a whoop, then instantly regretted it.

"You'd think this water would be warmer, considering the mountains are several miles away, and it's the dead of summer."

Morgan dipped a toe in tentatively. She rubbed her arms in her light shirt then waded in, frozen. "It's not that bad," she said through chattering teeth. "I don't know what you're complaining about."

He splashed at her, and she choked back the icy water before splashing him back. "Hurry up with the soap so we can get out of here."

He swam over to her and dunked her head underwater. She sputtered but came up laughing. He put his hand on the small of her back and pulled her closer, his long hair dripping. She smiled and ran her tongue across the front of her top teeth in a tease.

Jayden splashed at her playfully, accidentally sending a massive wave toward her with magic. She choked on the water and splashed him back with equal intensity.

"Be careful! There won't be any water left if you keep barraging me like that."

"Me?" Morgan said in mock hurt. "What about you? I knew I should have stuck with teaching you explosives. You are far better at that than doing anything else." She laughed, receiving another splash to the face.

She felt a rumble that shook the water and her with it. She began mindlessly scrubbing at herself. When Jayden handed her the soap, she almost didn't register him. It took her another few minutes, but she finally finished and headed for shore. She never stopped looking toward the direction of the camp.

"I felt it, too," Jayden said.

It almost seemed like he'd replied out of a dream. "I'm sorry, what?" she said, still not looking at him.

He jerked her arm. "I felt it, too."

She turned to him, shaking her head as if coming out of a trance. "Yes," she said, starting to smile, "do you know what that was?"

He shook his head.

"It's Brenna and Alaina," she explained. "They're looking for me."

She dashed out of the river, shaking her mane of red hair and letting magic do the rest of the drying off. She picked up her clothes and started running. She could hear splashing from behind her and called back to Jayden. "You'd better follow my lead, or headache be damned!"

Morgan barely registered the thumping of his feet behind her as she dashed toward the camp. Her newly cleaned legs were steadily becoming muddier, but she didn't stop.

When they ultimately made it back to camp, Morgan grinned and announced. "It's only a matter of time now before we're ready."

Erra suddenly rushed in, waving his arms wildly. "They're coming. I saw it." He was out of breath, but green light circled his frame like an aura. "Zachariah's disciples are just beyond the gate."

The smile slipped from Morgan's face. Suddenly grim, she turned to find Jayden still wet, though clothed. She nodded at him. He nodded back. "Sibyl, take Erra, Fabian, and Elsie to the frontlines. I'll follow in a moment."

Everyone nodded resolutely and hurried to their designated positions.

Morgan entered her tent and began to dress, putting on a corset and skirt that cut to her thigh. The rest of it draped down about her legs, long enough to cause distraction but slit enough to fight with her legs if she had to. She tied a band of leather around her thigh for her dagger's sheath. Her mouth remained in a firm line as she stuck the knife inside and bound it shut.

Jayden slipped in behind her. He grabbed her hair and started weaving it in a plait against her back. She said nothing, only allowing him to continue.

After a few moments, she said, "It's too soon. They came before we were fully ready. I should have noticed it sooner."

"Yes, you should have," Jayden agreed, finishing the braid and tying it with a strip of leather string.

She turned to him only briefly. "No time for jokes now."

"In all reality, then, you should shut up and head to the frontlines with me. You talk too much."

Morgan glanced up at him momentarily before heading out the tent door, Jayden already a few steps ahead of her.

"They're ready," he said flatly after a moment. His strides were long, but he didn't sound out of breath.

"I'm not so sure of that."

"Trust in your people. You gathered them for a reason. They aren't there to keep your spot warm."

Morgan exhaled quickly and picked up the pace.

They entered the clearing in an explosion of dirt. A shot of fiery gray had just whizzed past Sibyl's head, and she was making a creature in the air. With a burst of burnt sienna orange, a lion formed and charged at the group of Zachariah's Dark Ring. Several of the followers scattered, but an unfortunate disciple was ripped to shreds. It evaporated.

Fabian generated lavender bolts of lightning and sent licks of them hurtling toward the advancing army. A private storm was brewing, and his cloak whipped in the increased wind of his tornado. The cracklings of thunder shook the ground.

Elsie's turquoise fire formed into whips that she lashed at the Dark Ring. Each time she made contact with a shield, sparks flew. Their gray powers whistled harmlessly by each person, eventually crashing into a dusty heap.

Morgan simply stood in awe, staring at her coven and the protections set in place. It was working. After 300 years of striving to make their home safe, they had finally done it —they had finally found a method that worked. She looked up at Jayden, who also stood in awe, drinking it all in. Finally.

"The spell we put in place," Jayden said under his breath.

"It's working," Morgan finished for him, her hands coming up to cover her mouth as a tear trickled down her face.

EIGHT

Fight

SOMETHING WAS WRONG. MORGAN STOPPED FOR A MOMENT to feel the beating of her magic. It was like the sound of a heartbeat in her head. She scanned the battle scene to see the lights of gray fading. Each member of the Dark Ring was turning, one at a time, running away into the forest. They'd won, right?

The aching in her head persisted and began to grow stronger with every pulse. She turned to see Jayden experiencing it, as well. His head was slanted, his eyes lost in a distant gaze.

Fabian, Sibyl, Erra, and Elsie had all stopped in confusion. They, too, were scanning the horizon to see what was happening. The red barrier Morgan and Jayden had put up earlier was still holding steady, flickering with sparking red energy like a net.

"What is—" Jayden started.

Suddenly, a wave of fear crossed her mind, destroying all thoughts but one: My sisters.

She didn't even look at Jayden before she tore away

from the scene, crashing through the underbrush as she ran. There was a piercing pain in her head, but she ignored it, too focused on the feeling of dread that came from her sisterly concern. Brambles threatened to take her down, but she kept moving, picking up speed the longer she ran. It was all a blur.

Noah and Caleb were back at the site, she knew. Were they dead? Injured? Fleeing? No, she couldn't imagine they would do that. After all, they were Alaina's and Brenna's mates. Inevitably they wouldn't run. Would they?

The pain in her head subsided slightly, and she heard Jayden crashing in the growth behind her. She felt the sting of an impact in her gut, but she daren't stop to check.

"Get in the car!" she screamed at Jayden, slamming the door behind her in the Infiniti QX50. She let her magic flow freely as she clutched the steering wheel and turned the key. The engine burst into life, and she hit the gas pedal, swinging wide and missing trees only by blasting them out of the way.

She lifted a finger to the ceiling of the car, making it flash silver for a moment before expanding to envelop the entire vehicle. Jayden cried out in alarm as the floor of the car began to disappear. "What are you doing?"

"We're vanishing."

The car went careening through the trees, crashing over large rocks and tree stumps. Morgan could feel his confusion at their safety.

"You could be helping me!" she shouted at Jayden.

He stared at her in return. "You want me to start blasting away at these trees with what I've learned. Are you crazy?"

"Just do it!" She leaned forward enough that her chin nearly rested on the steering wheel. Brambles and branches were bashing at the car's windshield, but she pressed further on the gas pedal, pushing through them all.

Jayden had his head out the window and occasionally spluttered as pine needles, and summer leaves whacked his head. He was attempting to incinerate some of the obstacles. Still, the spells kept missing, crashing into the ground and spitting up dirt and mud.

"If you do that one more time, I'm going to murder you in your sleep!"

"You won't have to," he managed to say before another onslaught of branches slammed into his face. "If you keep driving like this, neither of us is going to make it out of here alive!"

Morgan groaned in exasperation and grabbed the back of his shirt, pulling him back into the car. "Take the wheel," she said, climbing over him. She still had a firm push on the gas pedal with her red magic, forcing them onward.

Jayden took the wheel in a craze, swinging wildly and nearly causing her to fall out of the car.

"Watch it!" she shouted as she forced the ground to smooth in front of them. "I swear. have you never learned to drive?"

"It's on the agenda!"

Finally, they were past the worst of it and onto a paved road. Jayden had a death grip on the steering wheel when Morgan swung back inside.

"How can a car this old go this fast?" Jayden asked, never taking his eyes off of the road.

Morgan lifted jazz hands, her mouth firming into a thin smile. She sat back against the plush interior and heaved a sigh. "It's not more than 15 miles away. If you step on it, we might be able to make it before Monday."

He turned to her with a look of disgust. "You are mean when you're in a hurry."

She stuck her tongue out at him, then stared back at the road. "Now, you're going to turn left here, got it? In 500 feet. 300. 200. 100. You're going to miss it!" She grabbed the steering wheel from his hands and jerked to the left. The massive boat of a car used its only asset to stay on the road: weight.

Morgan felt herself flying to the right, but she held tight to the steering wheel and planted her feet firmly on the other side of the car as it lifted up on two wheels. She slammed on the brakes with her magic, and they squealed to a halt, landing once again on four wheels.

"That's it. Get out."

"What? No! We're going to lose time if we do that."

"I don't care," she said flatly. "You are terrible at driving, so up, up, up."

Jayden got out of the car, flabbergasted.

"Now, I can't go anywhere without you, so either climb into the passenger's seat or hop on top of the car." She drummed her fingers against the steering wheel in irritation. "Let's go!" she said exaggeratedly as he took his time to walk to the other side.

He fiddled a bit with the door. "I can't see where the blasted handle to this thing is!" Morgan opened the door with her foot and pushed it open. When he was finally backed in the car, she hit the gas pedal again, forcing it to the floor. The tires spun for a moment, then grabbed ahold of the dirt road and sling shot them forward.

"What is the point of a speedometer if it won't register anything?" Jayden shouted above the roar of the engine.

"I'd like to think it's a good decoration," she said, equally loudly.

"Can't everyone in the whole country hear us?"

"Nope. Dampening spell."

"Then why am I SHOUTING EVERYTHING?"

"I like a car with a good roar to it." She grinned over at him, and then winked.

They reached a clearing in the trees, the direction they were headed blocked by a large cliff face. Still, Morgan kept driving toward the rock. Jayden said nothing, only shaking his head slightly and blinking slowly.

"What is it?"

"Since I've never been here before, but I've seen Batman movies in the past, I'm going to assume that we are going to drive right through it, and I don't know if I have the stomach for any more surprises right now."

Morgan laughed and hit the gas. They zoomed through the bluff side into a dark cave only dimly lit with lanterns. The roar of the car lowered substantially as they continued to drive.

"Why is the sound getting quieter when we're in an enclosed space?"

"Because I'm trying to listen, stupid," Morgan hissed, sticking her head out of the driver's side window. There were very few sounds, only the occasional voice. Morgan's eyebrows furrowed. "I can't hear anything—"

A blast erupted by their car, obliterating the vanishing spell and pushing them against the wall.

"This is my favorite car," Morgan said through gritted teeth. She pushed her way out of the window and sent a spark of red light into the dark cavern.

Up ahead, another blast echoed through the chamber, blue light mixing with black, the black magic seeming to eat away at the color in the darkness. Blues and yellows mixed with various shades of green, but the black bursts snuffed out the lights in the corridor one by one.

Morgan cautiously opened Jayden's door and beckoned

him to follow, crouching. They crept through the darkness to a larger chamber filled with stalactites, dripping quietly. At the center of the cavern stood Brenna, with her mate sending out whips of blue-green light into the swarming mass. One man had his back to Alaina, creating a storm of yellow-green about them. Alaina stood with her hands raised to the sky, a ball of yellow flame held high above them all.

Seth had a band of disciples with them, all sending streaks of black into the storm. They launched explosive spells at the group, but Brenna's shield of blue erupted in a cloud, sending bits of the cave flying about the room. Morgan stared in awe at the scene. Either their regeneration had sparked this incredible increase in energy, or they had been studying extensively while away.

The two men seemed to fight in hyper speed, their arms moving in quick motions. When their feet hit the ground, the cave shook, and Zachariah's disciples fell to the earth in unison.

Morgan sent up a shield of her own, in red, but it fractured quickly. Then, Jayden was beside her, holding his arm parallel to hers and recovering the fractures with another burst of red. Morgan looked over at him and smiled. "On the count of three, then."

Jayden nodded. "One... two... three."

They stood as one and sent a wave of red through to Zachariah's disciples. Both Jayden and Morgan blocked the light from their eyes and charged into the fray. Grabbing her sisters and their mates by the arms and tearing them away from the fight.

There was an explosion of white light as the six escaped. Morgan held fast to Jayden's hand as they headed back into the tunnel. When they reached the car, Morgan gently nudged the dings back into place and corralled everyone inside.

"Nice to meet you," Morgan said as she put her right hand behind Jayden's head and started back up quickly. Once they exited the bluff side, Morgan turned the car and hit the gas. "Next stop, headquarters."

NINE

Bounded Mates

"We've just met," Morgan yelled over her shoulder. "I know one of you is Caleb, and the other is Noah, but I don't know which is which."

"I'm Noah," the dark-haired man said.

"And I'm Caleb," replied the other man, red-haired.

"And, who's…?"

"I'm mated to Brenna," said the red-head.

"Ooh, watch out," Morgan said teasingly. "She'll take a bite out of you, that one."

"And I see Jayden's the new boy toy," Alaina said in a drawl. "I'm surprised you didn't come to pick us up in a VW van, to be honest."

"That's it," Morgan yelled, leaning over the seat to take a whack at her sister. Jayden pulled her back to the steering wheel with one hand while trying to steer with the other. She glowered over at him but begrudgingly returned her hands to the wheel. "You little smart-aleck. I'll get you when we finally arrive.

"Alaina, things have been so crazy, I haven't gotten the chance to hear more about you. It's been over 300 years since I've had a conversation with you about your life, and it's been more than that since I've wanted to talk with you, Brenna. Tell me a little more about Caleb and Noah."

Alaina offered a kind smile before turning to Noah. "This is my mate. We've been together for nearly three weeks. I'm sorry we didn't have the chance to get caught up back at camp, what with the injury and all."

"Closer to four," Noah said with a wink. Alaina only laughed.

Alaina elbowed him hard in the gut, making him cry out softly.

Finally, they were pulling into the wooded area of headquarters. The rumble of the car became a dim hum as they pulled up beside the tents and came to a stop.

"Brenna," Morgan said, turning to look at her sister. "Where were you since we last saw each other?"

"Grand Meadow," she said simply. "I met Caleb at psychiatric facility. He rescued me. We've been together ever since."

Alaina scowled at her as she patted her hair back into place. "And what of you, Morgan?"

"Oh, making up for past mistakes, I suppose," she said, though she was lost in thought.

Mrs. Dougherty dipped a cherry into chocolate, letting it settle on her lips for a few moments before seductively sucking it into her cheeks. "So," she said, once she had swallowed and spit out the seed, "do tell of what I have to be afraid of?"

Morgan must have appeared to wear rags compared to the lavish apparel Mrs. Dougherty sported. She cast her eyes downward, trying her best to appear presentable by flattening the wrinkles in her skirt. It must be a nervous habit, she thought.

"Yes, as I've said before, Zachariah is relatively close, and he is dangerous. If you could leave your estate for more than a week or two, we should have this settled by then."

Mrs. Dougherty leaned forward, showing the crests above her corset and offering a knowing smile. "Is there something you want of me, my dear? Why else would you come in the strangest of times?" She reached for another cherry and dipped it daintily.

"Oh, I'm sure it's nothing you can't handle. My master just wishes to clear the house before there might be fire upon it. You understand."

Mrs. Dougherty leaned back against her cushioned seat and gazed warily at Morgan before smiling once again. "If you would send your master to speak with me, I'm sure we could come to some sort of arrangement."

"You don't understand, my lady. He is yet a few days' ride from here. I came ahead to make sure everything was in place when he came." Morgan tried her best for a smile. "Mrs. Dougherty, Claudia."

Mrs. Dougherty turned up the corners of her mouth slightly, closed her eyes momentarily, and shook her head.

"Mrs. Dougherty," Morgan corrected. "You understand my position at this point. I can't send for him while he is yet on the road. There is no way for me to reach him."

"I'm sorry," Mrs. Dougherty said, rising from her seat. "I'm afraid there is nothing I can do to help you if I don't have the advice from your master directly. Now, you have been very helpful to me the past few weeks about the house, but there is no way that I can comply. Good day." She gave a brief curtsy before disappearing into a large archway behind her.

With no other way to persuade her to leave, Morgan exited the house in trepidation. It had been over 200 years since Zachariah had first taken the power of the Stone. He had laid waste to almost everything in his path, and she had received word that he would be here next.

Here.

Morgan looked back at the house in desperation. There was

nothing more she could do but meet him on the road. Morgan mounted the horse and headed east.

She remained in a forested area for many days before she saw him come. He had a following behind him, some ten disciples. Taking a breath, she emerged from the area to stand in front of him.

He had corrected his drooping skin from the last time she had seen him. However, his eyes still burned as black as coal in his head. He seemed to leave scorch marks where he walked, and as he stopped to stare at her, his boots continued to sizzle slightly.

"Well, my love. It has been some time since I last saw you. I'm surprised to see you here now." He smiled that extra-large smile, though now his cheeks seemed pinched.

"I can't let you go further. You know that."

He tapped a cane against the ground, sending a shower of dirt toward her face. She only blinked and thrust a hand to the side, sending up a block. He continued to smile as he glanced around at his disciples. They looked like beasts when once they were men.

"I see you admire them," he said, gesturing to the group around him. "It took me some time to train them, but they... adapted." With a small whistle, he sent every one of them toward Morgan.

She jumped high in the air, somersaulting over them to land next to Zachariah. "Don't do this," she pleaded. "Remember once when we planned to live alone in the hills of the Americas? Remember once when we wanted to have a family?"

His smile turned to a sneer. "That was never my dream." He whistled again, and the disciples came back, brandishing balls of gray fire. They shot at her, but she dodged, using a heel kick to send a burst of red energy toward them, felling them effectively.

Zachariah's sneer turned to a knotted frown. He struck the ground with his cane again, sending sparks of black up from the earth, threatening to capture her. She jumped, sailing in a backflip over to the minions and slashing their throats with a blade of her magic. He looked angry for the first time, lashing at her with black lightning.

"Don't forget," Morgan said as she raised a shield. "I'm the one who trained you, and I'll be the one to defeat you."

He laughed as she sent a stream of red bolts toward him. Zachariah intercepted them with his cane and sent them careening toward the earth. Black tendrils eased from behind him, underneath his cloak, and lashed at her like whips. She spun, creating a tornado about her, sending the blackness lurching in different directions. With a side kick, she sent a red knife toward him and caught him in the chest.

He faltered, and then fell to his knees. Morgan drew a knife and advanced, never taking her eyes off him. He choked up blood—no... blackness—as she advanced. She refused to shift her gaze from him, though now he seemed helpless.

Once she reached his body, she extracted the knife and held it to his throat. "Give me a reason not to kill you." Though the words came out like daggers, she felt mercy for him. She moved her knee to his chest and pressed him into the dirt. Just as she was about to plunge the knife in, he opened his eyes. Not the black eyes he had from the Stone, but his green eyes, the eyes he'd had before he'd fallen victim to it.

She hesitated.

As fast as they had appeared, they were gone, and he struck her with his black magic, sending her tumbling. Lifting a hand to her head, she felt a trickle of blood. She shot him with two daggers of energy, pinning him to the ground. He remained there as she lashed him with magical bonds. She transformed him, then, into a key.

As she sailed for the Americas, she felt the pitch of the ship as it hit the waves. The cold spray of ocean water stung her eyes as she dug the key from her pocket. "Never again, my love," she said to the key under her breath as she tossed it into the sea.

She stared down as it hurtled through the air, watching it transform into him again, though unconscious. She looked away before he hit the water.

Jayden pulled her from the car behind him, clutching

tightly to her arm as Alaina, Caleb, Brenna, and Noah continued to talk in excited tones. "I noticed that."

"What?" she asked innocently, trying not to dwell on her feelings of unease.

"Something's bothering you. You never told me. I didn't know he was once your lover."

"He wasn't." Morgan turned away from him, clasping her upper arms with knuckles that had just turned white. "Not really."

He stood next to her and wrapped his arms around her from behind. She tried to break away, but he held on, resting his chin on top of her head. After a moment, she stopped struggling. "I don't care if he was, only the way he's connected to you. I don't want you falling into trouble because of it."

"Our relationship had never been simple, even before he used the Stone. At first, he was my student, then my friend, then my… well, you get the idea." She paused for a moment and stared into space. "I just don't want this to be like last time."

"You mean with Kian?"

She nodded stiffly. Whenever she felt free of the guilt for teaching Zachariah, she felt the cutting shame of letting Kian die by Zachariah's hands. She couldn't remember the last time she wasn't racked with guilt about the whole thing. Sending her witches to protect the front-line while it was her doing that sent them there. The ache when someone in her coven died because of her negligence.

"It's different this time. You've got me."

This time, she did break free to turn and stare at him. "What difference will that make?" she asked through a forced laugh. It was the only thing that kept her from crying. "I told you about Kian. From what I can surmise, you've read my mind when it came to Zachariah. None of that made any difference. Even with my sisters with us, I don't see how that could make any difference." She put a crooked finger to her lips then stared at the sky, praying for her tears to fade.

"It's love. That has to make a difference. Alaina has Caleb, Brenna has Noah, and you have me. Though I might not be as magically strong as Zachariah, I can put up a decent fight. And I'd never give up on you." He walked to her again and put his arms around her, burying his face in her long, curly hair.

I hope you're right, she thought, her mind becoming dangerously clouded with doubt.

TEN

Through His Eyes

ZACHARIAH WAS SITTING ON A THRONE OF WICKER, THOUGH IT *wasn't that. It was something else, blacker. The dark walnut of the chair became oily and slick as it continued to move, as if in vines. He sat at the top of a small crest, looking over the valley below.*

Beside him were his creatures of the black. They knelt and crawled along the ground around Zachariah, bellies to the ground, occasionally glancing up before continuing to move. Their fur glistened, though there was very little light in the night sky. The fur—no, a series of dark slug-like creatures clinging to their skins—vibrated with every muscle movement. The beasts made hissing noises out of their noses, their faces caught in an endless sneer.

Zachariah's disciples had gathered near. His face, though still mildly resembling the man Morgan had once known, now was pale and pointed. The jeer painted to his lips seemed somehow stuck, as though it had not fallen for years. He stared at them as they began to chant in low tones.

They began to gyrate slightly, lifting their hands to the sky and swinging their bodies back and forth.

A woman was brought to the center of them, bound and gagged. She had a look of terror on her face and more than a few bruises. It appeared as though she had been merely beaten, though. Zachariah must have wanted a purer sample, not soiled by his followers.

The chanting became louder as he descended from his throne, wearing a cape of black mist. Seth emerged and presented Zachariah with the Stone and a dagger, the same dagger he had used to pierce Morgan. Seth bowed deeply, never meeting the eyes of his leader. Instead, his gaze remained fixed on the ground.

Zachariah took the dagger and the Stone gently, moving in concert with the chanting that still echoed through the trees. He lifted them high above the head of the woman. Her eyes grew wide, and she tried to scream but couldn't.

With a resounding crash, he brought them down hard upon her stomach. The light slowly faded from her eyes as orange magic began to seep down her torso. Zachariah bent low and inhaled deeply, the magic becoming a part of him. The disciples continued to chant in rising tones as he breathed deeper.

Soon, all of the magic was gone, and the witch remained in a shriveled husk on the sacrificial table. Zachariah closed his eyes and extended his arms, letting out a chorus of the chant himself. After a moment, he opened his eyes and stared right at her.

△▽△

MORGAN WOKE FROM SLEEP, drenched in sweat. It was only just beginning to become light outside. The morning birds chirped melodiously as she sat up. Incredibly, Jayden was still asleep. She didn't know how he could remain so peaceful when she could barely catch her breath. She put a hand to her head and grimaced.

Jayden remained silent on the ground in his bedroll as she stood from her cot and wandered outside. The sun sent rays through the trees. Morgan grabbed a blanket from her bed, wrapping herself gently as she breathed the clear morning air. She put her hand to the ground and felt the rumble of the earth beneath her.

It had been over 300 years since she had left Zachariah on the moors of Scotland. It almost seemed like a dream. A terrifying dream. She pulled the blanket closer as she stared at the ground.

Zachariah was getting more powerful all the time, so they had to attack soon. With the six of them, they might be able to put a dent in his army, though it was hard to tell at this point. The best chance they had was to draw him closer and hit him at home, right where their protections were. It was the only option.

Of course, she knew that he would follow her. He had so many times before. Still, it bit at her insides to realize that where once there was love for one another, now there was animosity. Hatred. Still, he was connected to her in a way that no other had been.

It was time for that to end.

Jayden lifted the tent flap to glance at her through bleary eyes. "What are you doing up so soon?"

"I think I've got a lock on him," she said without looking back. "I felt him in my dream last night, and I know he felt me. It's only a matter of time now until he comes to get me."

"Well, that's very bleak."

She snorted breathily. "I lead a very bleak life." She started to draw on the ground with a small branch. "We have to get the Stone from him."

"The Stone of Obscuras."

"That's right."

"What's so special about this stone? Does it do tricks?"

"No," she said through a laugh. "It takes your power and combines it with the powers of those that possessed it before. If you've practiced with it enough, it becomes a tool for extracting the power of others. Usually, that comes with a spell or some sort of sacrificial artifact. It looks like Zachariah is using some kind of dagger to do it, though I don't know what kind. I don't usually make a habit of studying dark objects."

"I see. And he plans to do what? I know he thought he'd killed you a few weeks ago, so he can't be after you. Is it your sisters? Does he just want to wipe out the known world?"

"A little bit of both, I think."

"That's dark." He rolled onto his back and stared at the canvas top of the tent. "I don't know if I could do something like that."

"It gets easier if you think you're doing it for a good cause."

"And what cause would be worthy of that?"

"A home." She looked up at the rising sun again, drinking in its rays. "A home where no one wants to hurt you. A home where you can feel safe and warm and not have to be afraid of someone discovering your secrets. Somewhere where you could set up camp, have a beautiful house with indoor plumbing"—he snorted, but she ignored him—"and people that will accept you for who you are."

"That sounds like what you have now," he said, grabbing a strand of her long hair and pulling it gently. "You know everything except the indoor plumbing."

She chuckled under her breath. "Can you imagine if I just integrated myself with the world, what others would think? You grew up in this environment, so you know what magic is like. But for the average person, it might be too much to bear. They might go back to old traditions, such as burning at the stake or dropping you down to the bottom of a river with a stone attached to your ankles saying if you drowned, you were innocent. If you lived, you were a witch, which got you killed anyway."

"It sounds like you've had some experience with that."

"I've been thrown under the water a time or two. Of course, the secret is to wait for several hours before reemerging, just to be safe. Then, you just move on."

She threw the stick on the ground and stood.

"You might have found some peace if you'd taken the Stone yourself."

"Maybe," she affirmed. "It certainly drew Zachariah to it."

"So, what's the next step?"

"The next step will be in his possession. He's had it since the day he took it, though not always on his person. Now, though, he probably won't go without it. If he loses it, he loses himself."

"What does that mean?"

She smiled back at him. "I have no idea, but aren't you excited to find out?"

When Brenna and Alaina awoke, they sat by the fire as their mates massaged their shoulders. "Lucky," Morgan said under her breath, and immediately Jayden came up behind her and started poking her with a stick. "I thought I was muttering about a massage, not asking to be a human dartboard."

"Shut up. You'll get what you get."

"Brenna, Alaina," she said between pokes, "you two and your guys will draw the disciples off as Jayden, and I sneak in. It might take some time, but I need you to direct him over to that cavern." She pointed to a rock face in the distance. "Once there, Zachariah will slip in and try to take me first. I believe he wants my magic most of all. At least, he wants me dead. It should only take a few minutes for the four of you to batter them enough to join me in the cavern. By then, he'll be trapped.

"Remember not to take him on without assistance. His stone is designed to sap your magic, so you'll have to use some fancy footwork out there and keep an eye on each other. The pairs you four have made should give you enough power to punch through his defenses while I use Jayden to go for the stone under the guise of my invisibility spell."

He stopped poking at her and dropped the stick to his side.

Morgan turned to him. "You're up for the challenge, aren't you, Jayden?" She flashed him a smile as he glowered. "As soon as you have the Stone, we'll destroy it. Easy enough, right?"

Brenna looked skeptical. "Surely there's another way to go about this. It seems as though you're putting an awful lot of risk into this. Jayden is not fully trained, and you're just now using your powers at a greater capacity. Maybe it should be Noah and me to spearhead the attack."

"No," Morgan said flatly. "He's after me. He has been for over three hundred years, and he'll hardly be satisfied attacking one of my sisters. No, I have to take this one on."

"But what if you die?"

"So be it." Morgan stood straight and nodded stiffly. "Whatever it takes."

"All right," Alaina said, standing. "Call him.

ELEVEN

Recovering

Morgan and Jayden meandered away from the group, claiming they needed the fresh air to calm their minds in preparation for the battle. Of course, they really needed the mental strength to proceed.

Morgan felt an ever-increasing need to be with Jayden. Over the past few weeks, they had not only been close, but they had also been inseparable. They had to be physically near each other, but it was becoming much more than that. He was strong, confident, yet humble about his abilities. It was more than she had expected from him, though she couldn't say it was all that surprising. He had impressed her many times over the last few years with his generosity and willingness to help, but only recently had she accepted it. He was becoming more a part of her so quickly.

They continued to walk in silence for over an hour, scouting the terrain in theory, but feeling a need to be closer to each other physically and mentally. The fresh forest air calmed their minds slightly, but they would need more than that to become one with each other, to truly mesh their magic together.

"I felt you worrying before," Jayden said quietly as they climbed a hill. "I know how you feel about going up against Zachariah. Even though it was a long time ago, they stay with you." He used her own words.

"Yes, I guess that's so."

They continued to climb at a steady pace until they reached the crest of the hill, where they sat next to each other, cross-legged. After a moment, Morgan leaned her head against Jayden and uttered a bated sigh. It had been some time since she had been this close to someone, this incredibly aware of what he thought.

He smoothed her raging red hair to the side and planted a kiss on her forehead. After a while, he rested his chin on the top of her head and wrapped his arms around her. She let him do it, ultimately sinking into his embrace. The sun was falling, and their spot above the tree line allowed them to see the full colors of dusk covering the land below.

"I'm not immortal anymore."

"I know."

"I could die in this fight."

"I know that, too."

She heaved a sigh but didn't move. Without their intimate connection, she may have thought him indifferent, but she knew better. The fight was likely to take both their lives, so there was no need to dwell on the issue. Instead, it was a moment of peace between them, as though death were a peaceful solution to the battle instead of a dreaded conclusion.

"I don't have to take you with me. In fact, I could find a way to sever the bond between us, and you could stay here."

He laughed softly. "What, and let you have all the fun? There's no way I would let you go out there alone, even if you wished it. It's more important to me that I'm there with you, be it through death or life."

"You're crazy," she said, sitting up and gazing into his eyes. "But I like that about you." She leaned in for a kiss, something she had previously sworn herself against. But, as time went on, she began to realize it was more likely for her to survive the fight leading up to her confrontation with Zachariah with a dose of love on her side.

He took the back of her head lightly and pressed his lips to hers. Though they only lingered a moment, she felt a surge of peace. Death was far sweeter an outcome now than it had been years before. Immortality suddenly didn't feel so important. She still had her magic about her, and Jayden was ever-present to take away the sting.

"Must you be so dramatic," he asked after a moment. "It's likely we won't have a scratch on us after this debacle, let alone death. Besides," he said and leaned forward again to kiss her lightly on the cheek, then on the forehead, later on, the nose, "there's nothing wrong with a little danger to spice up an otherwise dull life."

"That surprises me, coming from you," she said. "I thought you'd had enough danger to last yourself a life-time. It seems to me that you've been dealt quite the disas-trous hand, more than you probably should have."

"Eh." He took his hand from behind her head and leaned back on his arms. "We all face some danger in our lives, be it intentionally or not. That's the cost of living. And the cost of living sometimes comes with unfortunate outcomes. That doesn't mean that we should stop fighting, merely that we should stop trying to force fate's hand."

"You know, you are remarkably wise for someone so young."

"And you're remarkably pessimistic for someone who has lived through what would kill others."

"You get used to it," she said, brushing a hand under her nose. She stared off into the sunset again, the pinks of the skies fading into deep blues. "I've seen too many failures to optimistically say that I can defeat any obstacle that comes across my path."

"Yes, but you have defeated every one so far, haven't you? I mean, you're still here, still fighting."

"The demons inside me would tend to disagree with that."

"Then to hell with them." He looked over at her and smiled. "Morgan, it feels like I've known you my whole life, and though that is just a blip in how long you've been alive, it's certainly made a difference for me. You are not just a product of what others have done to you. You are not even a product of what your inner demons have told you. You are a product of your actions, and they are quite noble."

"Be careful." She glanced over at him with a tilted smile. "You make me out to be some sort of saint."

"Oh, I definitely wouldn't go that far."

She laughed despite herself, and he followed suit, first glancing at the rock on which they sat and then to her eyes.

"But I would say that you have a sort of fantastical connection with those around you," he went on. "Something that binds you not only to the earth but to the people that love you. You may find my opinion limited, but, in my opinion, those people are few and far between."

She blushed, and then brushed it off. "I don't know how smart it is to simply fight him while you sneak about the cave. Though that sounds like the most likely of plans and maybe the best one yet. I can't put my finger on this setup, but something seems wrong about it."

Jayden stared at the setting sun, his eyes starting to mist. "Maybe that's not the best way," he said quietly. "Somehow, I feel like there's something wrong, too. It's the most obvious answer. If he knows you're alive, he will suspect that you are baiting some sort of trap for him, and he'll bait you with a trap in response. No," he continued, raising a hand after she tried to interject. "I know exactly what you're thinking. For some reason, I can see what you saw last night—those creatures around him and the sacrifice. He didn't have the Stone on him at the time. Seth had it with him."

"Which only makes sense that he would keep the Stone with him, knowing that I saw that, right? Ah," she exclaimed. "This hurts my head."

"What if he wanted you to see what he saw for a reason? I know you didn't see it through his eyes, but he stared right at you. There has to be some reason for it. He must have known something. Maybe he just wants you to think it on his person when in fact; he's hiding it somewhere else."

Morgan turned to him, skeptical. "You really think there is something to that? I mean, sure, he stared right at me at the end, but Seth had the Stone on him at the time. Maybe he's just trying to confuse me."

"Come on," he said, pulling Morgan to her feet. "Let's go ask Brenna and Alaina what they think."

"You only want to ask other people because you want to confuse them with your lunacy."

"You just don't want to talk to them because you know I might be right." He lifted his eyebrows several times, and then dragged her down the hill.

They whipped by branches and shrubs, never breaking their handholds. Morgan laughed underneath her breath, trying not to let Jayden know how he excited her. After a while, though, she figured it a lost cause and burst forth in laughter. "You're going to take me out through these trees."

"Then you'd better hold tighter." He started to pull harder, and Morgan sealed their grip with magic, and they thundered through the trees.

At last, they made it to the camp, out of breath and puffing. "Good heavens," Brenna said, pulling both of them down to the fire to sit. "What has gotten into you two?"

"It's got to be at a secure location, right?"

"What is this about?" Alaina said, entering with her usual haughty air.

"The Stone. He's got to know that we would expect him to have it, right? I mean, he's gone to great lengths to make sure that Morgan knew he had it."

Brenna, Alaina, Caleb, and Noah looked quizzically at Morgan. Finally catching her breath, she recounted her dream. Brenna and Alaina looked at each other in fear, and then turned back to Morgan. In a flash of rage, Alaina yelled, "Why didn't you tell us?"

"I don't know. My mind has been so fuzzy the last few weeks, with the binding, that it hardly seemed like reality. It wasn't until Jayden read my thoughts and saw it too that I finally believed it was something."

Alaina looked shocked, and then turned away, heading back to the fire. Brenna laid a hand on Morgan's shoulder. "What makes you think he doesn't have it with him? Did you see it put in another location?"

"No, but he'd hardly show me that, would he?"

Brenna sat back, pulling a large kimono tightly around her waist. She looked upset, shaken. She only nodded for a moment before starting to pace slowly back and forth in front of the fire. "But what of the plan?" she asked eventually. "Do you think he knows of the plan through your connection with him? It seems unlikely that you would be able to hold much back from him, considering his rising powers."

"If it has been compromised, we would surprise him by going to his hiding place for the Stone. There would be little danger in letting me and Jayden head out for reconnaissance for the time being."

"Morgan," Alaina said, hands clenched into fists. "Have you no thought for anything else? You have used your connection to call for him. No doubt, he is on his way here right now. And what if your plan fails? What if you and Jayden are gallivanting off in the middle of nowhere, and he comes to attack us? Huh? The three of us can use our magic more effectively together, you know that. You might get this whole coven killed for the sake of a hunch."

"It's hardly a hunch," Morgan said quietly, red anger rising to the surface. "And what if we're right? What happens then if we do nothing? If the Stone is in some other location and we stay here to fight Zachariah, there is no way for us to defeat him. The only way to kill him is to take the Stone of Obscuras from him. I tried it once before. He'll regenerate again and put us back in this same position, without a hope, and without a prayer."

Alaina stalked off with a disgusted groan. Brenna watched her go for a moment before turning to Morgan. "I don't know about this."

"I know," Morgan said, her anger fading. She reached out to grasp Brenna's hands. "I know, but if we don't follow through on this, it could mean the death of us all. If we don't at least check it out, we could be in for a world of hurt, and one of us could end up dead."

Brenna only nodded grimly.

TWELVE

Inside

THEY BID FAREWELL TO MORGAN'S TWO SISTERS AND THEIR mates and headed out into the night. Somehow, this didn't seem as frightening as facing off with Zachariah in a one-on-one battle. Of course, she wasn't sacrificing the most important part of that plan: Jayden.

The Infiniti QX50 bumped along slowly through the night. Neither of them knew where to go. The dream that had seemed so vivid earlier seemed fuzzy now; images that had been as clear as day when she'd experienced them faded slightly. She could no longer make out the faces of the disciples. The background of Zachariah's wooden throne clouded.

Morgan crinkled her brow as she struggled to remember the details. Maybe there was a town in the background. Perhaps it had been merely a forest. She couldn't tell for sure.

She absent-mindedly guided Jayden down various streets, pointing out landmarks that may have been landmarks. Still, there was no definite in any of it.

The night sky sparkled as they made their way onto open

roads. Soon, however, the lights of a nearby city obstructed their view, and the passing street lamps blocked out the stars. She began to feel tired. They had been driving for two hours, three, maybe four. She couldn't keep it straight anymore. The ground whisked by beside her, and she soon became mesmerized by the constant shades of gray whipping past.

Her eyes began to close. She shifted uncomfortably in her seat, trying to rest her head against the most comfortable part of the window. The plush leather seats folded her in, and she quieted down the roar of the engine to a gentle purr.

△▽△

FLASHES OF LIGHT, of sound. Zachariah grinned broadly as he poured inky magic into a disciple's mouth. The minion gagged but kept his mouth open, deceiving his mind by closing his eyes. When they opened again, the whites of his eyes had turned black. Zachariah ceased the endless flow of black magic into his disciple's mouth.

The disciple began to convulse and fell to the ground, lying spread eagle. His tremors increased dramatically as the seconds passed. Black started to gush from his mouth, nose, and ears. A lump began to form at the center of his throat. It swelled as it throbbed, looking as though his skin was about to burst.

Finally, a pinprick of a wound appeared on the lump, and black and red blood poured from it, quickly dispelling the lump but covering his body from head to foot in the vile liquid. He continued to convulse for another few minutes before lying limp, his eyes still open in horror.

Zachariah kicked him in the side, with no response. "Another!" he cried over his shoulder, and a long line of witches appeared from the blackness.

Seth led the group, pushing forward to the front of the line and standing with his chest puffed out. "I'm next, my lord." He willingly knelt before Zachariah, opening his mouth and closing his eyes in anticipation.

Zachariah had long since lost regard for human life, even when it came to his most trusted ally. So, he didn't hesitate, reaching behind him and grabbing the Stone in one hand, the other floating lazily above Seth's head. Zachariah didn't chant, only gripped the Stone firmly, letting his own blood mix with his black magic.

The free hand descended with finality at the pinnacle of Seth's forehead. Seth flinched slightly but made no other movement. Zachariah lifted his hand and placed it over Seth's mouth, beginning the procedure again.

Like the last, Seth fell to the ground and began to convulse, though less aggressively. Black magic still poured out of his mouth, ears, and nose, though not at the same rate. His hands were clenched tightly in fists, and his muscles strained in his neck. The same lump momentarily appeared, and then disappeared just as quickly as it had arrived. After a moment, he stopped convulsing, the black magic flowing less freely from him.

Zachariah stood over him, releasing his hard grip in the Stone. He waited for some minutes before striking him again.

Seth stirred slightly at the kick but made no noise. After a moment, he sat up straight and opened eyes black as night. He stood as if lifted by a puppeteer, his body at a right angle to Zachariah. He seemed strange, as though there was no life remaining in his body. He seemed only an empty shell of a man.

Zachariah spoke in a soft voice, obscured, unintelligible. Seth turned his head only. It appeared as though disconnected from his body. He continued in silence as he began to move across the room and knelt before a stone altar, not moving a muscle.

Zachariah grinned broadly. It looked as though his flesh barely stuck to his face like it had been plastered on and clung to the bones only out of habit. He furled his cape of black magic about him and walked to the altar. Pulling Seth from his bowing position, Zachariah held his hand over the altar. He took the Stone in a vice-like grip and cut a gash in Seth's waiting palm.

Seth made no noise of pain nor showed any inclination to leave. Instead, he stayed in his rigid, bent position and let the blood flow. But it wasn't just blood. It was the same stuff as before, that same crude black and red that had leaked from the other's disciple's neck. Instead of oozing thickly, it flowed down to the top of the altar, appearing to singe at the faintest touch.

After a moment, the altar made a loud, rumbling screech and began to fold in on itself in triangles. The first few appeared to be little more than puffs of dust erupting from the opened crevice, but as the hole grew larger, so did the triangles. Red mist rose in a huff around the opening. Seth's blood continued to pour like gelatin into the hole. Still, Zachariah kept his hand rigid over the surface.

Once the altar had opened to a diameter no larger than a foot, Zachariah tossed Seth's hand to the side and gently placed the Stone inside. His hand clear, the opening shut like a trap in the same way it opened.

△▽△

MORGAN WOKE WITH A START. They were still on the road. Still driving after who knew how long, though it was still dark.

"It looked gray," she said, opening and shutting her eyes rapidly, trying to regain clarity.

"What did?" Jayden looked half asleep, himself.

Morgan glanced at the clock. Half-past five in the morning. They had been driving all night. "The building. He must think I'm little threat if he's letting me see so much about where he is."

"Or, he could think you're back at camp with your sisters, and he's preoccupied with something else. Open your mind for a minute. I want to see."

Morgan shut her eyes dutifully and let Jayden invade her thoughts. After a moment, she opened them again to look at him. "Well, what do you make of it?"

"I don't see what you see. The gray building? I don't know that I could have picked that out from that vision. Do you think maybe you were thinking about the altar?"

"No. I can't explain it, but the building felt gray. It was like I was looking from the outside in, and I could feel the structure around me. I know that sounds stupid."

"It does," he agreed, but he didn't laugh. "Did you have any more revelations while you were under?"

"None that I can speak of, but I feel like we're going the wrong way. We should head back the way we came."

Jayden didn't argue or make any movements in disagreement. He pulled over to the side of the road and flipped around carefully. "This car of yours certainly has no easy way to turn around." The boat-like tilt of the car made him grip tightly to the steering wheel. "Also, don't you think we're a little conspicuous in a car nearly 100 years old?"

Morgan nodded absent-mindedly and put a finger to the top of the car. It began to ripple in streams of silver before once again disappearing around them.

"I'll never get used to that. It's too unnerving."

But Morgan wasn't listening. Though her eyes remained open, she maintained a far-away look fixed beyond the road. "Come on," she said under her breath. "I know I can find you." She closed her eyes hard.

Zachariah laughed beside her, pushing her hair behind her and leaning forward. A kiss. She was lost in it—the way he felt on her lips, the way he brushed her cheek with a thumb, the way he made her spine tingle as he pressed her close to him.

She opened her eyes again, but her eyes remained bleary. She shut them again, clearing her mind.

He pushed her to the ground, deepening the kiss. It was more than an afternoon stroll now. "I love you," he whispered in her ear. She could feel his hands caressing her cheeks, her neck, then taming her wild mane of red hair still blowing in the breeze. She felt his mouth open to hers, and she felt herself giggle, though it seemed an out-of-body experience.

Morgan kept her eyes closed as she continued to remember what only seemed a few weeks ago, not 300 years. "Come on, my love," she said under her breath. "I can feel you near me. I know you can feel it, too. Remember me."

He moved his hand down to her waist and gently stroked her side. She could feel his smile through their kiss. "I love you, my love."

"I know," she said, pulling in closer, her hands running through his curly black hair. "I'll always love you."

She opened her eyes suddenly. "Gotcha."

He strolled through the gray building out to a forest, pines. When he looked to his right, he saw a gravel parking lot. To his left, he saw the driveway leading to the main road. There were no other buildings in sight, just the one he exited.

Zachariah turned to look at the building. Its basic structure was rectangular, but slashes of gray concrete streaked the side, showing imperfect window structures. The door was made of slate gray and looked to be a work-man's door, unremarkable. Trees secluded the building for the most part, though it was located reasonably close to the main road. He blinked.

△▽△

MORGAN GASPED and clutched at her seat, her back lifting from the cushion. After a moment, she lowered down and smiled, turning to Jayden. "He's so near, I can feel it. And I saw it. The building. I swear we passed it before I fell asleep. That building was so unusual. It looked so plain when we passed it, but only now, after seeing it through his eyes, I don't know how I could have missed it."

Though Jayden looked exhausted from the night of driving, he nevertheless kept his eyes open and alert as they headed back toward camp. Light peeked over the edges of a distant mountain, and the light blues of morning took over. They were nearing the end of it all, she could tell.

They stopped for a moment to collect their thoughts, trying to clear her mind by rubbing her temples. They needed to deepen their emotional connection for this to work. It would require a lot of heart on both sides for them to defeat Zachariah in the end. They stretched their powers through a ritualistic dance, both of them moving with the magic they felt, perfectly in sync.

"Are you ready?" Morgan extended her hands next to him and felt him move in kind.

"As long as you have some semblance of sanity, I guess I do, too." He grinned over at her then broke the rhythm to grab her about the waist and raise her off the ground. Morgan giggled and put up a fighting effort to release herself, though she enjoyed the comfort. He continued to twist her around through the air until, after a few moments, he released and kissed her.

She could feel the red magic shared between them begin to pull them closer together. Though he was by no means a professional at the craft, if they remained in emotional and mental sync, they might just pull this off.

"We should contact Brenna and Alaina. It's not too difficult, just put your forehead to mine and concentrate."

She ran her finger through his hair and pulled his head closer to her own. Magic kept them bound together as they stood facing one another, eyes closed.

"First," she instructed, "enter my mind. See the connections in my brain and feel yourself meld with them." She felt him probing her mind again, her thoughts quickly transferring over to him. She smiled. "Good. Next, reach out to Alaina and Brenna with your mind. Access the memories both you and I have with them. If you are struggling to find a connection, latch onto mine."

Morgan adjusted her weight, standing more centrally in front of him. She could feel Jayden reaching for the memories, but roughly. "Easy," she said, beginning to sense the same turmoil in her own mind. "We want to make a connection with them as easily as possible. They should feel it just as easy to connect with us as we can with them."

Suddenly, her mind shot into Jayden's and through his body. She could see his heart beating faster, though she felt the compensation he tried to make by breathing in slow, deliberate breaths. His anxiety tore through her mind, but she began to lose her calm.

"Easy," she said again, though she didn't feel it herself.

Their connection became labored, and she could feel the fluctuations of their magic begin to wobble. What once was a perfect sphere of feeling connecting the two was now contorted and pulsating. Morgan tried to break the connection but found herself glued to his forehead, experiencing the same levels of fear.

His breathing became more arduous. He began to pull at her mind, forcing the connection between them to fuse. She began to lose her sense of reality, lost in his mind. His grip on her tightened, and the magic that once flowed freely clenched them like a vice.

He was back in his village, before it had burned,

dancing with his sister as his mother and father laughed. A stranger came walking in from nowhere. He seemed strange, as though his skin was sloppily pasted to his face.

Then the fire, the roar of the flames, and the sounds of screams as Jayden's family succumbed to death after what seemed hours of torture. He stared at them, feeling the tears running down his cheeks, though they evaporated quickly with the heat. The suffocating pressure of smoke on his lungs pulled him further down into despair.

Then, Morgan could see her own face fighting through the fire, a hand reaching out. He wouldn't move, so she took his hand and pulled him from the burning building. Everything was fire, even her hair. It was difficult to stay standing, but she seemed an angel, despite the soot on her nose.

Morgan pulled away after a moment, finally able to release when their memories combined. Jayden had tears in his eyes, though he quickly wiped them away.

"It's all right now," she said, though choked herself. She grasped his cheeks and forced his eyes to meet hers. "It was a long time ago, and we can care for each other now, huh?" She smiled gently, tilting her head. "I know you're afraid. I am, too. But we're here for each other now. All it takes is a little faith, and we can get through this."

He fell into her arms, shouldering away the sense of anxiety he felt.

Though taken aback, she put her arms around him and buried her head in his shoulder. "It's going to be all right," she kept repeating. She still felt the anxiety he had projected, but he began to calm, and she began to believe her own words.

Eventually, she pushed him back by the shoulders and stared up at him. "You're going to have to trust me on this. Just like you did before. Do you think you can do that?"

He nodded solemnly, his eyes dry.

"We have to do it again, and no," she interjected when he opened his mouth to protest, "I'm not going to do this on my own. We shared something special in our connection just now, and the only way we're going to succeed is by trusting each other. And you need to trust that you can do this. Come on." She took the back of his head and placed it against hers again, starting the connection once more.

This time, she gauged his emotions and memories, interjecting her own thoughts as a guide to him. His breaths were still shaky, but he managed to hold on through the bond. The connection flared between them, and Morgan could feel the red magic, forcing both of them to glow slightly.

"Talk to them," Morgan said breathily. Jayden took another unsteady breath then began to speak. The call was direct and straightforward. "Now, show them the image I showed you of the building."

He was hesitant, shaky, but he searched for the picture in his mind. When she felt his instability, she pulled him back from the brink, directing his thoughts to her vision. Brenna and Alaina nodded in the affirmative and disappeared from the connection.

"Right, let's go." Jayden headed toward the car when Morgan stopped him with a pull on his arm.

"It's all right, you know. To feel like you've lost control sometimes."

He nodded once, his face sober, and turned to the car again.

They rode in silence for the next hour, but she allowed Jayden to probe her thoughts. She kept her hand locked in his, and red energy swirled from their fingertips. She let her eyes drift closed as she listened to the hum of the car. Sun shone through the invisibility shield, and the warmness of his hand in hers created a sense of peace she hadn't felt in many years.

Though she had been in love before, there was always some reservation, some part of her that refused to truly give all of herself. Perhaps it was the fear of living with a mortal while immortal herself. Maybe it was the fear that somehow their connection would be broken. But, when she looked at him, she felt at home. After years of dragging herself through the countryside trying to find a way to defeat Zachariah, it was almost a relief that someone was with her, perhaps near the end of her life.

They closed in on the building she'd seen in the vision. Just as they had been in her mind, the sides of the building were slicked gray with jagged diagonal creases of cement crossing the windows and door. The enormity of the situation weighed heavily on her heart, and it was all she could do to keep a straight face when glancing at Jayden. For all she knew, this could be the end of the line.

Morgan felt the needling sensations of fear and excitement, anticipation, and peace. Zachariah was really after her. He had been for over 300 years, and he would be until she was dead. It was impossible to see any other outcome.

It seemed a kind of release to realize she might not walk out alive. It would be over. After she had helped to create the monster that killed for sport and pleasure. She had let him gain power when perhaps she should have killed him before he'd made it across that lake. There was a sense of honor in sacrificing herself for the sake of those she loved.

Brenna, Noah, Alaina, and Caleb all stood in the shade of the pine forest, each emitting their own glow of magic. Morgan turned to see Brenna looking at her peculiarly, concern was written across her face. Morgan smiled at her sister and headed for the door of the building.

But before she could take more than a few steps, Brenna ran to her and pulled her to the side, guiding her toward the looming forest. "I know what you're thinking."

"Oh, Brenna," Morgan said, patting her arm and offering a bleak smile. "You can't really stop me at this point. It's gone on for so long now, and I'm tired."

"No, you are not going to get yourself killed to fulfill some sort of imagined debt you believe you owe these people. Can't you see that there is more to living than dying?"

Morgan pushed Brenna away from her, her smile turning downward. "There's more to it than that. Don't be ridiculous. Zachariah could have thousands of creatures at his disposal, waiting to tear into us. I'm not just doing this for me."

"Yes, but imagine what would happen if we did lose you. If we combine our magic together, it'll be more powerful than if it was just Alaina and me. Think with your head for a moment." Brenna poked Morgan on the forehead, hard. She began to breathe quickly, but Brenna wasn't known for tears. "If we lose you, it could mean the death of Jayden, not to mention the rest of us."

Morgan stood back, stunned. Of course, she had thought of the implications that might happen if Alaina and Brenna were down one sister, but she hadn't considered Jayden. He was still so young.

She nodded solemnly. "Then, I'll need your help."

"That's why we're here."

THIRTEEN

The Chamber

ALAINA WAITED NEXT TO THE DOOR WHILE CALEB SIDLED over to her side. She brandished yellow fire at the end of her fingertips as she held an attack position. Brenna quickly sprang to the other side of the door, blue magic dripping from her hands. Both Caleb and Noah stood in front of the door and ignited their colors of chartreuse and cyan, waiting for a command.

Jayden was next to Morgan, some distance from the building. Though he was still new to the powers, he ignited his fingertips with red, glancing over at her only to nod.

"Whenever you're ready," Caleb said, not turning from the door.

Morgan took in a deep breath then exhaled quickly. "Now."

Noah and Caleb sent bolts of their magic to the door, blowing it open and revealing a dark entrance. Though the rising sun lit the building leading up to the door, it stopped at the opening. Only blackness could be seen within.

Morgan gave a mental nudge to Jayden, and they both

entered silently, hands ablaze. They had just made it inside when the door slammed behind them.

The faintest whisper of breath echoed through the chamber, extinguishing their flames. Neither of them moved. Neither of them dared to. After a moment, they reached for each other and once again lit a red flame in their entwined fingers.

The darkness seemed to consume everything. Even the glow emitting from their hands was not enough to cast light onto their faces. "There must be some sort of spell," Morgan said in a hushed whisper.

Jayden sniffed audibly. "Do you smell that?"

Though faint at first, she did notice the increased stench. The longer they stood in one place, the more pungent it became. It smelled like something rotten and something scorched. She couldn't place it.

"Do you know where it's coming from?"

Morgan felt his conflict, though he didn't say a word.

"Perhaps we should keep moving."

Carefully, they drifted forward, only inches at a time. "What happened to the door?" Jayden was interrupted by the sound of a footfall slipping on the ground: his own. "What—"

Morgan forced the blaze to ignite the room with light in a flare. The brightness temporarily blinded them, but once the light returned to acceptable levels, Morgan's chin dropped in horror.

Beneath them were the bodies of hundreds of people, all emitting blood and other bodily fluids from their noses, mouths, and ears. Most of them still had their eyes open, while some no longer had eyes. It looked as if the eyes had exploded, leaving a stain of red covering the veins that led to their eye sockets. Many tongues were swollen and purple, while others appeared to have swallowed their tongues.

Each body was bloated. They looked to have been dead for several days, though it was impossible to tell. They were haphazardly stacked, creating a massive pile of bodies near the center of the room. Morgan held her breath to keep from gagging.

"What... what is this?" Jayden sounded horrified, and a quick glance in his direction showed his hand to his mouth, eyes popping.

"It must have been something to do with the Stone. Like I saw in the vision," Morgan said, trying not to cough. "Though I didn't know he'd killed so many people. I only saw the one."

The gray building no longer seemed a safe house for Zachariah and his disciples, but rather a mass graveyard for the bodies he had discarded after experimentation.

The flare of red that lit the room began to fade, and Morgan caught a brief glimpse of Jayden's frightened glance as the room went dark. "Do it again," he said agitatedly. "Send up a flare, or light some candles, or do something."

"I'm trying," she replied in desperation. Each spark she tried to light in her mind seemed smothered by the fog of black that weighed down on her magic, silencing them. Fear took over her mind, preventing her from thinking clearly. She blinked her eyes rapidly, though there was no need in the vast blackness.

A noise started softly from a corner of the room. Morgan's breath caught in her throat, and Jayden's hand tightened its grip on hers. It sounded like a scuffling like something was scraping at the ground.

When she remembered her held breath, she exhaled

slowly. The noise stopped. She held her breath again, only just allowing herself to whisper, "Don't move."

The scuttling started again, headed toward their position. Too afraid to think of the light, Morgan stayed locked, frozen, scared to even move. Another evil sound echoed, followed by a light trilling of vocals. What sounded like fingernails scraped against the stone ground. Morgan allowed a tear of fear and felt it slide down her face. It hit the floor with an echo.

The trills became louder, and more voices joined. The scraping of talons—fingernails, something—became quick and decisive. The scratching no longer seemed searching, inconsistent; it appeared to be directed toward them.

Fear clouding her mind, Morgan reached out in front of her desperately and came in contact with something hard. She squeezed. It began to ooze in her hand, and she barely held back a scream.

Jayden was suddenly beside her, grasping her arm in an unyielding fist. His other hand clamped around her mouth, perhaps just in time. For a moment, the sounds stopped. He finally spoke under his breath. "For heaven's sake. Turn on a light."

Screeching sounded from all around them. Morgan clamped her hands to her ears and willed all of her power into him, too afraid to think. He began to radiate red light, like a light bulb just about to burst.

Across the pile of the dead lay, a creature shrouded in black with hollowed eye sockets. The creature's white face gleamed like a pearl but otherwise stayed perfectly still. "Did you see that earlier?" she asked Jayden in a voice barely above a whisper.

Jayden peered at it. "It's not moving," he said. "Maybe it's just something we missed earlier. We could have mistaken it among the dead."

"I don't think so." She barely dared move. The effort it took to breathe seemed excruciating.

"Let's go around." He was still glowing, still emitting that foreboding red light that had once seemed a color of safety.

She caught his arm, still staring at the eyeless thing whose black face seemed a maw. "Wait. Jayden, if that's one of the dead, why is its face turned up like that?" She inched closer, wondering what ill-gotten power seemed to draw her to this creature. Morgan carefully stepped over the bodies of the dead, her eyes never leaving the pearly face. She leaned into her front foot and a bone cracked beneath her heel.

As she looked down, she heard the sound of scuttling again and flicked her eyes back to the face, but it was gone. Dread filled her as she desperately searched around the room for it. "Where's it gone? Where is it?"

Her fears turned to anger as her head swiveled, but the thing was gone.

"We have to keep moving." Jayden moved away from the spray of blood on the ground and started to saunter away. Morgan turned to him and saw it, there on his shoulder, the outlined, decaying face of someone long dead, its fingers like the bones of a wing turned to razors.

She screamed and lashed out with her magic, only to send Jayden sprawling into the dark ooze on the ground. The red glow faded slightly, and Morgan sent up a pillar of light, nearly burning her corneas. It scuttled away from him and disappeared into the shadows.

She felt her mind grow fuzzy as she drifted into memory.

It was the first time in a long time since she had gotten to know him that he was ready to increase his training. Zachariah had been a pupil of hers for only a few years, but he showed the most promise of anyone she had taught. He cast spells of flickering butterflies into the air, watching them flutter in shades of chthonic before fading into nothingness.

"So," she said, positioning herself close to him, "hold her hands in front of you and feel the energy in your gut. Once you feel it well enough, begin to form the ball of lightning, like this." Her own red magic began to crackle and shoot sparks, but she contained it, compressing it into a steady ball. She collapsed her hands and extinguished it. "Now, you try."

He gave her a quick peck on the cheek before forming his own ball of energy. Occasional bolts shot from its core, but he soon had it contained. His tongue stuck out like it always did when he concentrated. His face screwed and constantly rotated, never giving the same expression twice.

She laughed. "See, you're getting the hang of it." She created her own ball of energy again and shot it out into the green pasture. It created a significant boom.

That wasn't right. She made sure not to make it explode too close to where they were. If someone caught them, they would notice and perhaps do something drastic.

He brought her back. "So, what if we aim at a target? Like a barn, or at a cow." His face lit up in anticipation.

"We don't want to draw attention to ourselves. Besides, you know how I feel about killing things."

"Come on now. It'll be fun. We could even aim it at the sky if you want. Do you see that flock of birds above us? I'd bet we could give them a right good scare if we took a few shots at them." He grinned broadly and pointed upward. "Come on, Morgan. Have a little fun in your life." His skin began to fluctuate from its natural olive complexion to a pearl white and back again.

No, that wasn't right.

He snapped his fingers in front of her face. "Remember? The birds. We could just scare them. I know how you're fond of birds."

Morgan smiled, laid on her back, and began to form a ball of energy.

A slap resounded on her cheek, and she was back in the gray building among the scores of dead bodies. The door was open, and Brenna was shaking her. "What... happened?"

"That's what you get from drifting off in some memory. You were creating energy balls. Jayden kept trying to reach you, but you were having some sort of fit. He kept saying you were obsessed with the sounds of some creature. He said the two of you saw it for a second, and then you started attacking him."

Morgan looked over to see Alaina keeping the door open through a protection field of yellow. "We have to get it and get out of here."

"Yes. Now, show me where it is."

They walked over to the altar, stepping through the corpses. They stood over it for a moment, attempting to pry it open by interlacing their magic in a dark shade of purple.

The clattering of bones against the stone floor made them freeze again. Morgan began to breathe quickly, fighting at the terror she felt. Alaina heard it too, and to listen closer, she extinguished the glowing yellow field she had applied to the door. It shut with a snap, Noah and Caleb left outside.

The room became deathly quiet as once again, it plunged into darkness. The silence became thicker, breathing more difficult. All four listened quietly to the tomb in which they had become trapped.

"Don't panic," Brenna said in a shaky tone. "We were

able to blast through the door last time, so we can do it again. Besides, Caleb and Noah are outside, no doubt finding a way to open it again."

But the inky blackness felt more constricting this time. The air tasted of sulfur and sage, and the silence was deafening. Even when Brenna cleared her throat, it sounded choked, muffled even though Sousan was mere inches away from her.

Morgan began to feel pressure on her shoulder and cried out, clawing at it in desperation. There was nothing there. The occasional sound of bones or nails scraping against the stone seemed to come from another time. The endless torment of the creature taunting them with noise was the only sound that seemed real. Everything else faded as though in a dream.

Alaina snapped her fingers to ignite a small flame. It sparked but fizzled, much like the rest of their attempts at accessing magic. Everything seemed shrouded in a pressing black force.

The scuttling of the creature became louder, and it began to trill incessantly. Morgan cried out in frustration after several minutes and pounded her head with a closed fist. "Why won't it stop?"

She was losing her faculties again, moving into the realm of dream and forgetting her connections to reality. The crushing weight of the magic made her chilled, but still very much constricted. It was becoming easier to sink into a state of fear and let her body move to the sound of the beating of her heart, like a hammer in her head.

She had snuck out again to see him. He loved to stand by the wild rose bushes in the glen to wait for her as she went outside. He greeted her with a grin and lilies, bowing to her in his regal manner.

"Kian," she said, hardly able to contain her excitement at seeing him.

He caught her in his arms and swung her around and around, laughing with her and burying his head in her hair. He always loved the smell of her hair. He always loved the way she smiled. He always loved...

The sound of a branch breaking shattered their connection, and he put her down slowly. His dark brown hair whipped harshly in a wind that had suddenly arisen. "Who's there?"

A dark figure emerged from the tree line, hooded and shrouded in shadow. The figure said nothing but continued to stand near the edge of the forest.

Kian reached for the butt of his pistol and pushed Morgan behind him. "Well, who are you, then?"

Still, the figure did nothing. It did not move despite the rising winds. Its cloak covered the figure's entirety, and beneath the hood was equally shaded. The figure remained at the edge, making no noise.

Morgan reached for Kian. "Let's go. Never mind him. We need not concern ourselves with people who won't talk to us." She sounded flippant, though fear stole through her heart. She knew who was beneath the hooded mask. It was only a matter of time until he found her.

Kian remained staring at the hooded figure as if made of stone. Though Morgan tugged at his hand, he seemed mesmerized and incapable of movement. Using a bit of her own magic, she sent a shock through him, finally causing him to turn.

"Let's go." She said it with more finality this time. She often took the back seat with Kian, preferring he take the lead in their relationship, preferring some sense of normalcy. But now she tugged at him fiercely.

The hooded figure made a screeching sound and

reached large, white, bony hands to pull back the hood. The screeching wouldn't stop.

Again, she stood in the gray building, still with no light, but the screeching came from all around. She nearly added her screams to it as she struggled wildly to remember where she was when she was. The confining blackness had started to take over her mind, confusing her.

Alaina screamed over the sound, "What is that thing?"

Morgan stood stock still, feeling woozy. She couldn't summon the light, and the darkness seemed to become blacker by the minute. Every time she raised her hands to form an energy ball, she felt as though she was moving back into a fog, unsure of the line between reality and fiction.

"Morgan, what's the matter?" Brenna sounded distant, though every word she spoke was further away.

The screeching continued. Morgan reached a hand over to the altar for support. It was becoming fuzzy again. She could feel her own breath, though it seemed like it poured in and out of her like jam. She sniffled quietly, almost reaching for her nose with a hand.

"Morgan," Zachariah said. "I thought you loved me." His wicked smile became more pinched as time went on, as though his immortality came at the price of his soul. Still, he reached out to her in a kind gesture.

All around the two of them, explosions hit the ground, spraying magic and dirt into a fine mist. None of it mattered, though. She stood in front of him with a sense of dread at his appearance.

"Where is he?"

"What, you mean your newest fling?" Zachariah smiled a grin too broad for his lips. His skin tightened about his bones and pulled at his eye sockets. "I thought we cared too much for each other to find anyone else."

Morgan spits on the ground. "I know you have him." She wasn't afraid, though she had been many times before. Kian was too close to her for her fear. Only anger remained.

Zachariah waved a hand and produced Kian in a swirl of black. He was on his knees and looked as though he had been beaten.

"What have you done to him?" Tears of fury leaked from her eyes as she glared over at Zachariah. Red fire flashed into her hands.

His black eyes remained fixed on her, and his smile hadn't slipped. It grew wider as he saw her begin to tremble. "Remember, kill me, and you kill him, though I hardly think he has long anyway."

Shots of orange and green hit around them as Sibyl, Fabian, and Elsie rushed to the scene. Zachariah's own people began to flood into the region, fighting back against the onslaught of Morgan's coven.

Though it was years ago, she could still see Zachariah put a dagger to Kian's throat.

A flash later showed a trickle of blood appeared at the corner of his neck, but Kian remained strong, only staring at her.

Another flash and she watched as Zachariah pulled the knife across Kian's neck, his throat beginning to show through the skin.

"No!" Morgan screamed, sending a red burst of fire in front of her. It landed on Seth's chest.

It seemed to take forever for him to fall, though they immediately felt the consuming darkness begin to lift as he dropped to his knees. His eyes remained pointed forward, his face was gaunt. He landed stiffly on his side and rolled to his back.

Morgan strode over to him and pulled him by his

collar, her eyes meeting his. "I know you see me," she said through gritted teeth. "You sent your lackey to kill me when you couldn't do it yourself. The death of an innocent man is on your hands, and the death of this fiend you corrupted will forever sting you. Do you hear me? I know your black arts. I showed you how to communicate. Fool."

Seth's already black eyes went dead and Morgan gripped his wrist with a raging red hand and dragged him to the altar. "Knife," she said, without looking behind her. Someone placed one in her outstretched palm. With little care, she slashed open his hand and let the black-red ooze pour from his body onto the altar.

Once the altar began to open, she threw his body to the side and picked up the Stone with her bare hands. Though the blackness threatened to consume her own magic, she held it firmly and conjured a fistful of rock, burying the Stone deep inside. She opened the door to the building with a crash. The gray concrete began to crumble around her, but she continued to move, her sisters in tow.

"Get my car."

FOURTEEN

Time

MORGAN FELT THE CONSTANT SURGE OF RED MAGIC coursing through her veins. It was like a fire that rocked through her soul. Jayden sat beside her as they headed toward the main camp in her Infiniti QX50. At last, she felt that she was ready to take this on. At last, she felt ready to be rid of him. He had made a vital misstep.

Everyone was silent, though she could sense unrest. Noah and Caleb shifted uncomfortably in their seats as they occasionally shot glares of disappointment at Alaina and Brenna.

Once the QX50 pulled up to the site, the four scrambled out. Noah rounded on Brenna, already in fumes. "I can't believe that you stayed in there without my help, without consulting me."

Though usually the calmest of the three sisters, Brenna turned to him angrily. "As if I need your approval to help my sister. I didn't see you heading into the fray when there were screams inside. I didn't see you coming out from behind your fear to help Morgan."

"My biggest priority is you."

"And my biggest priority is my family. If you don't consider yourself a part of that, then there isn't much I can say about your character."

"You thought a little more of my character when I followed the ice queen to Uskye and remained there, living in the midnight sun while you soaked up the endless blackness."

"You really are an idiot, aren't you," she said through taut lips. "Isn't it obvious that I was preparing my mate to stand by my side when combating Zachariah? I've discussed this with you enough for you to realize how important this is. I'll not be bullied into believing that your selfish need to be near me somehow puts me in the wrong."

He clenched his fists, and bursts of cyan sparked dangerously. "So, what, you've been preparing me for was your guinea pig, is that it? That I would somehow be some pawn in your feud against your sister's rival?"

Morgan furrowed her brow and opened her mouth to respond but was immediately silenced by Brenna's raised hand.

"Do you know who we are dealing with here? Morgan trained Zachariah, but she was far from the reason for the feud. He took the Stone of Obscuras, one of the most powerful weapons of evil in this world. Do not drag her into accepting his failures as her own."

Noah was silent for a moment, slowing his breath. "Brenna, this comes from a place of care, not of hostility. I'm sorry for my outburst."

Brenna returned to her demure nature, any indication of her blue magic resuming a state of rest. She nodded stiffly. Though he seemed cowed, his nostrils still flared. He simply bowed and took Brenna's hand.

Jayden meandered over to Morgan, hands in pockets. "Well, that was embarrassing."

"Yeah," Morgan said under her breath, not looking at him. "My family can be a bit embarrassing."

"I heard that!" Brenna said, glaring playfully at her sister.

Alaina gazed at Caleb sidelong, her mouth firming into a thin line.

"What?" He jumped back, shoving his fingers into his own pockets. "I'll behave."

The silence after the outbursts gave way to distant detonations. "There's no downtime, is there?" Morgan asked, expecting no response. She grabbed Jayden's hand and pulled him toward the frontlines.

After so little sleep, she ceased to care if Alaina and Brenna were behind her. Jayden soon took the lead and pushed through, lightening with a red aura.

Once they reached the frontlines, they turned to see the rest of the group following, Alaina and Caleb in front with Brenna and Noah following closely behind. They still held hands, despite their previous argument.

Down below, Sibyl guided the attack on the Dark Ring, sending daggers of fire toward the enemy.

Zachariah paced at the edge of the protections like a cat, eyes never leaving Sibyl. He made no move to use magic, only grinning at her through the shimmering red barrier that wobbled with each attack. His lips were pulled back into a grin, and his gaze burned darkly. His eye sockets oozed his dark magic, which showed in stark contrast to his pale features. His cloak of black magic flurried behind him and went up in smoke at its base.

The Dark Ring continued to fire shots at the defenses, to little avail. Some of the attacks made it through the barrier, shattering it in places to be quickly rebuilt by one of Morgan's coven witches.

Brenna stepped forward, looked at Alaina and Morgan, and took their hands. "This is the most important part of your life, all right? We can get through this, but it will take dependence on each other." She beckoned the men to come closer. "We're counting on each of you to make this happen. It is vitally important that we are connected before we face Zachariah."

She broke their hand connections and pulled Noah closer to her. "I love you, and I have since the first time I met you." Her eyes glistened slightly with tears. Forcing them back, she continued. "The only way that we're going to make this out alive is if you trust me, all right? That means you have to trust that we can succeed, no matter the obstacles."

Brenna turned away from him to face the rest. "For now, everything is holding. Luckily, we were blessed with a sister that knew a little something about defenses, otherwise who knows where the rest of us would be.

"Alaina, your strength has always been your fierce desire to be right." Alaina rolled her eyes, but her cheeks reddened. "I'm serious. Without your ferocity, it's unlikely that we would have the energy to make it this far. Though we may not always see eye to eye, you have always been one of the strongest women I have ever met.

"Caleb, I only knew you for a short time before this happened, but I trust that you have our best interests at heart. Because you are mated to Alaina, there must be some stabilizing factor in your relationship. You'll need it before long. Alaina is the most volatile of us all, so it's your job to make sure that she continues to keep her powers in check.

"Morgan, you have been around Zachariah the longest. You know how he behaves and understands his next moves. That makes you the biggest target. Zachariah is more likely to take you down than any of the rest of us. Because of that, you need to continually be on your guard. Protect yourself against his dark energy since you are mortal now.

"Jayden, Morgan is not fragile, as you've no doubt guessed after spending over ten years with her. Still, she is prone to be too daring and is likely to get herself killed. Your chemistry is one of the best reasons I am sure that you two can fight together. You will have to combine your thoughts and emotions to work as a team to defeat Zachariah, but I believe you're up to the task.

"Love," she said, taking Noah's hand and looking into his eyes, "is the reason we can get through this. Without it, we have no way of pulling together to defeat him. Now that we're together, we are strengthened significantly with our powers. This is the first time in a long time since we've had this experience to be so close and to work together to take care of the world, but it's our turn now."

Brenna finished speaking and nodded solemnly.

"That's kind of corny," Jayden said under his breath.

Morgan silently agreed but had to stop herself from elbowing him in the gut. They indeed were a unique but able match. She pulled him to the side, eyeing Zachariah as she did so. "Are you ready for this?"

"Is there a way for me to answer that without sounding stupid?"

Morgan laughed breathily and looked down at the ground. "No, I suppose not." When she peered up at him again, she had tears in her eyes. "You know why this is happening, right? It has to do with me."

Jayden tried to pull her into an embrace, but she held out a hand. "You do have a large part of yourself invested in this because of what has happened, but that doesn't mean it's your fault," he said. "Do you understand that? If I threw myself over a bridge because you said I looked stupid with a fedora on, it would hardly be your fault, now would it?"

She laughed again, tears leaking from her eyes. "You would look stupid if you wore a fedora. It doesn't suit your huge head at all."

"Listen," he said, suddenly serious. "The choices that man has made have nothing to do with you, do you understand? He became a fool too obsessed with power, and you too obsessed with taking care of someone else. I know how you summoned him here. Hell, I know how you found out where the Stone was located. You're right, there's a part of everyone that never really leaves you."

Morgan felt a wave of shame, and her eyes shot to the ground again. It had been she who had trained him in the first place. It had been she who had given him the illusion of superiority due to his powers.

He lifted her chin and searched for her eyes. "That doesn't mean you are making up for a mistake. You didn't make it; he did. You gave him the love of a beautiful, powerful woman, and he twisted it. I know you have trust issues after that. I know you have problems letting me in. We're no longer just partners in this anymore, understand? We can become inseparable in magic and mind."

"I love you," she said through choked sobs. She was surprised to hear herself say it. It felt like news to her, but she couldn't deny it. She felt that, for once, she wouldn't have to worry about whom she trusted.

"I love you, too," he said softly. "I've loved you since the day you popped into my life and saved me. It may have been creepy at the time that a ten-year-old wanted to hit on you, so it might have been hard to mention before." She laughed again, imagining that shy boy she had saved. "But I'm here now. I may not be a witch, but you are, and that's how we can make it through this. Now, come on. Your sisters are giving me a weird look, and I prefer to stay on good terms with them, at least for the time being."

He grinned as he took her hand, dried her tears with the other, and pulled her back to the group.

She took a deep breath then headed toward the barrier, Jayden and the rest of them in tow. Zachariah was grinning at her, revealing bright, sharpened teeth, but Morgan didn't look away. Looking up at the barrier, she saw the sparkle of red reflecting off his ghostly face.

"Let's end this," she said, and she dropped the barrier.

FIFTEEN

Zachariah

Zachariah's lips curled back, and his eyes widened in anticipation. Nonchalantly, he strolled through the gap in the magic that started to fade on either side of him.

Morgan stepped back to let him pass, not taking her eyes off his. She could feel the support from Jayden fueling her power, making it pulsate in her hands. Despite herself, she gave a smile of her own, making Zachariah's lips spread further.

All at once, black magic shot in a tendril from beneath his cloak toward her head, guided by a pale white hand. She dodged, watching it pass her as if in slow motion. Another black tendril aimed at her legs threatened to take them off, but Brenna shot a blue bolt into it, making it shatter like ice.

Suddenly, the air was filled with black, oozing magic, lifting Zachariah off the ground, and shooting limb after limb of black toward the three of them. Alaina ran forward and planted herself in front of him. Grounding herself, she shot a wave of yellow magic into the ground, sending up a column of light into the air, which bit at the black, causing it to recoil.

With Zachariah distracted, Morgan sneaked behind him and sent daggers of red to his back. Zachariah roared, turning his skull-like face to her, his mouth now crumpled into a mass of skin that fell down to the base of his neck. Though his one hand fought against the burst of light from Alaina inching closer to him from the front, he reached his other hand behind him to pin her to a tree with black swirling about her face, choking her.

Brenna moved in, lightning crackling at her fingertips. But before she could land a blow, Zachariah's black appendages threw her to the side, forcing her against a rock face and sending her reeling.

Morgan managed to pull herself free and create a blaze of fire in her hands. It fizzed as it grew, sending out licks of light. She waited until it increased to the size of her chest before hurling it at the black pedestal in which Zachariah stood. It created a hole through the center, forcing him to nearly topple to the ground.

After a moment of recovery, Brenna sent a sheet of blue magic under the ground, freezing the surface.

Zachariah swayed, but more black tendrils erupted from his chest and shot to the trees around him, keeping him from falling to the ground. He snarled and sent a projectile to the earth, breaking the ice Brenna had created and sending Alaina and Morgan in a spin as they launched themselves from the ground just in time.

One of Zachariah's disciples attempted to throw a spell at Morgan, which she countered by sending a ribbon of magic at him, stabbing him in the heart.

Alaina began to rebuild her energy, and her blond hair began to crackle above her head, her whole body exploding with magic. With a burst, she threw her arms open, her chest out, and erupted with yellow energy, nearly blinding Morgan. Both she and Brenna hit the ground as Zachariah wobbled in his perch.

But, just like a spider, he began to crawl from tree to tree, black legs gripping at the branches. He no longer resembled a human, more like a creature of the night. Though the sun shone onto his face, it still seemed shrouded in blackness. He seemed to hiss as he moved from tree to tree, only holding on by the barest threads.

Alaina built up her powers again, creating a crackling thunder as she charged. Her shots at him came as high-beams, massively large and powerful. Morgan sent sharp spikes toward him, aiming to dislodge him from the trees, but the black ooze deflected each one. Brenna pulled lightning from the sky to hit the trees, sending shockwaves through the ground.

"Together," Morgan yelled, and the three sisters focused their energies, each pulling from themselves and the men. Alaina stood in the middle, and the sisters lined up on either side. Alaina sent a stream of yellow magic straight up. Alaina added to the fray with her own magic, turning it deep green. Finally, Morgan directed her energy toward the pillar, turning it a radiant white. Focusing the energy, Alaina sent a beam directly at Zachariah, missing him by inches.

Some of the black tendrils about his waist began to melt from the heat, lying helpless on the ground. Zachariah snarled and sent a series of black spikes at them. With a cry, Alaina spread her arms again, and the white light flashed from her, covering everything brilliantly.

The light faded slowly. None of the foliage had been affected, but all of Zachariah's Dark Ring lay on the ground, either dead or wounded, all of them unconscious.

The sisters let their powers enter their respective bodies again, feeling the energy coursing through them.

Morgan felt a strain on her magic and what seemed like a hook digging at her insides. She scanned the site, but Zachariah was nowhere to be seen. Still, the tugging of the hook inside her stomach grew. The pain intensified in her scar, where she had been stabbed weeks ago. She doubled over at the pain. Gathering her strength, she stood to her full height and looked above her.

Jayden was wrapped by the black ooze that now coated Zachariah. Zachariah had a knife cutting into Jayden's abdomen, in the same spot where Morgan had been stabbed. The vision had been a two-way street.

Brenna saw Jayden dangling above them and started to throw bolts of lightning at Zachariah, but he blocked them with Jayden's body. Each strike sent a jab of pain through Morgan exactly where Jayden was hit. She felt her magic start to fizzle every time there was an impact.

"Stop!" Morgan shrieked, clutching her stomach in pain. "Stop! You're killing me!" She put a hand to her face, feeling the sting of a lightning strike. When she pulled away, her hand was covered in blood. She willed herself to heal quickly, but every squeeze Zachariah administered to Jayden opened yet another wound.

Jayden looked as though he was going to faint. Deep welts appeared where the tendrils wrapped around him. He breathed shallowly, as though trying to control his pain.

Zachariah grinned broadly and flicked his eyes toward the other two men, standing next to a large rock in silence. Two black daggers formed at the end of a tendril of his dark magic, and he hurled them at Caleb and Noah, causing them to fall to their knees, impaled.

Brenna and Alaina likewise dropped to their knees, screaming, though Morgan couldn't tell if it was in pain or heartache. Their magic fizzled at their fingertips as they reached toward their two men.

"Now, my love," he said mockingly, "give me the Stone."

Morgan stared back up at Zachariah, her expression growing hard. Love is a weakness, she had said. Love is a weakness. Time seemed to become slower, and her gaze darted from her sisters to their mates, to Jayden. Love had seemed a weakness. It was what was killing her. It was what tore her sisters apart when they saw their mates pierced with black magic. It was what tore their lives apart—being dependent on someone else.

Being dependent on someone else. She peered up at Zachariah and Jayden, still suspended above them all. Finally, she smiled, almost imperceptibly.

Gathering her magic, she put every ounce of it into communicating with Jayden. Their minds connected, and he began to breathe slower. I need you to listen. Can you hear me?

Jayden gave the briefest of nods.

I need to pay attention to what is happening around you, all right? Let me know if you sense movement from Zachariah.

Won't he recognize this? Jayden asked.

Just trust me. If we stay on this channel, he might not be able to hear us or interpret what we're thinking. Don't pay attention to what I'm doing. Stay focused on what I'm saying. It might confuse you. Hold on. I know it hurts, but hold on.

Even through his thoughts, he sounded pained. He didn't nod or show any indication that he'd heard her. Perfect. Morgan knelt down with her sisters as tears rolled down their faces. She looked up at Zachariah again and yelled in frustration.

All right, she thought. I'm going to transfer my magic to you, okay? You'll have everything, so I won't be able to help you, but I trust you. Do you understand?

Yes, he said, sounding strained.

He seemed frightened. Morgan once again turned her face to the ground and fell onto one knee. It'll be all right. You know what you've studied in the past? Just keep holding onto that for me. She felt his affirmation. Good. When you receive the magic, pull it in on yourself. Feel that fire inside you and build on it. Take the pain from your mind and focus solely on exerting the magic outward.

Morgan slowed her breath and bowed her head. She felt the moist soil beneath her fingertips and gripped it gently. She had never transferred her magic before. She didn't know what it would do to her, what it would do to him. Since they were connected, she could get a general idea of his strength, but the sudden change in magic might be deadly. Quelling her fears, she put her head to her knee and began to transfer the rest of her magic to Jayden.

It felt as though every inch of her body was being sucked from her. Like her very soul would seep through her skin. She could feel her red fire moving along the channel she had created between the two of them. Morgan felt like she was drying up from the inside out. Still, she continued to send her magic to Jayden, gritting her teeth through the pain.

Zachariah shifted in the treetops, tucking the knife back into his garb and sending a tendril of black to wrap around Jayden's neck.

Morgan felt the pressure of the black magic around her own neck. She almost cried out but stopped herself just in time, pushing her magic to him as quickly as she was able. She felt weak as the last bit of her magic pulled from her body, and she collapsed on the ground, staring above her.

Jayden began to glow red, the magic bubbling the tendrils of black constraining his body.

Zachariah looked astonished, staring at the red magic Jayden emitted. "What—" he said, the skin of his face once again turning to a frown and pooling near his neck. After a moment of the sizzling magic, Jayden was released as the black magic constricting him fell to the ground in large globs. Erupting as clouds of smoke once they hit the forest floor.

Jayden landed in a squat, still radiating the magic. Though clumsy with the finer nuances of forming magical energy, he sent bolts of fire toward Zachariah, who began to flee.

In the confusion, Alaina and Brenna ran to Caleb and Noah, lifting their bodies and pulling the black magic daggers from their chests. Remarkably, both were still alive, though wounded. Each dripped blood in a steady stream; both were unconscious.

Brenna created a seal with her blue magic while Alaina lifted her hands high in the air and sent them crashing down, forcing the men's hearts to beat strongly again, taking them back from the brink of death.

Morgan lay on the ground, every inch of her body in pain. She turned her head to glance over at Jayden, who was sending a never-ending barrage of red magic at Zachariah. She tried to smile, but even the barest of movements seemed impossible. She was so incredibly weak.

Zachariah had begun to recover when he headed toward Jayden. His body no longer existed. Black magic had consumed him so much that he became whatever it created. Its arms came crashing toward Jayden, reaching with daggered ends.

Jayden pulled a mandrake root from his pants, crushing it into a fine powder before he sent it hurtling at

Zachariah. The impact sent Zachariah spinning backward, the black ooze hugging close to his body and retreating into his skin.

Morgan moved her head slightly to see Brenna and Alaina again. Both had sealed the wounds of their companions and pushed magic into their bodies. Caleb coughed blood until it became a clear liquid. Noah's breathing, once rapid and short, became deeper and steadier. Convinced of their recovery, Brenna and Alaina stood, gently pulling their mates to their feet and slinging the men's arms over their shoulders.

Jayden came running to Morgan, who barely felt the strength to breathe. Closing his eyes, he pressed his hands onto her chest, red magic flowing from him and into her blood again. She gasped as though suddenly brought back to life. While still aching slightly, she could move again. She got weakly to her feet and put her arm around Jayden, whose frame suddenly seemed massive.

"You did it," she said softly, throwing him a half smile. "I knew you could do it."

"Yeah, you always did have more faith in me than I did."

Far away, the ground began to rumble, and Zachariah exploded from the ground, sending dirt and plant life flying. He was larger than ever, his face no longer saggy but utterly bereft of skin. His large, black, popping eyes surveyed the six of them as he continued to grow. He was no longer human, no longer bound by the rules of reality. It seemed as though his life was no longer dependent on the flesh.

Morgan pushed off of Jayden and forced her magic to prop her up. Magic again began to radiate about her body, restoring strength to her limbs. Brenna and Alaina walked to her side and bent into attack positions. Their lips curled back in snarls. Morgan smiled as she glanced at them both. Finally, the three of them stood in unison.

Jayden stepped behind Morgan and put his arms around hers in attack position. She raised her arms to match his. From behind them, Caleb and Noah joined the fight, cyan and cerulean raging from their hands.

All of them moved forward as Zachariah sent a wave of black magic toward them. Alaina and Caleb held it off with a shield while Brenna and Noah began to shoot magic at the base of the black wave.

The pressure from the black magic bowed the shield, so Morgan and Jayden pushed up as well, forming an orange dome. Morgan felt her feet begin to slide and noticed the same of the rest of them. She whooped, bent her knees, and pushed off the ground, forcing herself into the air and pushing the magic shield with her.

The blanket of black blew apart, and Zachariah stood solidly, staring at them with piercing eyes. Just as he was about to gather his magic, Alaina, Morgan, and Brenna formed a shield around him with blinding white light. Zachariah fought against them with shots of black hitting the white, but the shield continued to hold and shrink.

The shots of black magic became weaker and weaker until they slowed down to several minutes apart. Morgan looked over her shoulder at Jayden, beckoning to him with a shake of her head. He stood behind her and put his hands on hers. She transferred the magical burden to him, maintaining the white barrier.

She turned away from them all for a moment and pulled the ball of stone from her pocket. Using quick slicing methods with her magic, she opened the sphere and poured the Stone into her hand. Black magic swirled as smoke around the glistening, translucent Stone. Again, black magic attempted to enter her hand through her pores, but her red magic held it at bay.

Morgan turned again to the white sphere that trapped Zachariah. "Let him go," she said, loudly enough to make every head turn. None of them questioned the command and released the hold, though each kept magic ready at their fingertips.

Morgan walked up to Zachariah; now back to a human form. He breathed shallowly. His piercing blue eyes had returned, and the black magic that had once enveloped him was now but a shadow. As she drew closer, he looked up at her through the corners of his eyes, never lifting his head.

He looked old, far older than anyone she had ever seen before. His face was no longer pulled tight but hung, sagging around his bones. His limbs had lost their constitution, making him look bony. He had so wanted immortality, and this is what it had done to him.

She took pity on him as she stared down at him. He was but a fragile version of what he used to be. She could still see the blue eyes that had once compelled her to train him. She could see the aging hands that had once caressed her cheek as she'd kissed him. She could still see the beauty in his features that once made him irresistible.

But now he was broken, a husk of his former self. Black magic had taken his soul in exchange for power. She had once wanted so badly to have fought by his side, all those years ago.

Morgan crouched down and held the Stone in front of his face. "It was so long ago that you took this from Scotland and ruined your own life. It's hard to believe what you traded that day."

He continued to stare, not blinking at her. All of his fight was gone. The only thing his face conveyed now was fear. She didn't know if he dared not speak or if he couldn't. He remained lying on the ground, motionless.

"I still love you," she said, just loud enough for him to hear. "There are always bits that remain. But this has to end, and you've had enough for one chance at immortality." She raised the Stone to eye level, then clenched hard, forcing her magic to crush it.

With an ear-splitting squeal, the Stone shattered, and Morgan let the pieces float to the forest floor. As she stood, Zachariah's body turned gray as it solidified into stone.

Morgan swept a tear from her eye before turning back to the group. Though she felt relieved, it also bit at her core to know what she'd done. She turned to the sky to prevent further tears from falling, and then strode into Jayden's arms. It was finally over.

SIXTEEN

The End

Morgan walked hand in hand with Jayden away from the site, gently wiping her nose on a long sleeve, her eyes downcast.

"It was more difficult than you thought?"

Morgan looked up at him and smiled sadly. "Yes, it was harder than I had anticipated. There was still a piece of him in there, though it had been corroded over time. I guess there is always part of you that remains, either in yourself or in other people."

"He hardly seemed the type you'd take home to your mother."

She remained serious as she thought about that, finally responding, "He was, once."

Brenna and Alaina had rushed back to base camp with Caleb and Noah, each taking care of their men to make sure they had fully recovered from the bout. There would likely be scars for the rest of their lives.

"Do you ever wish you had spent eternity with him?"

"Sometimes," she admitted, still not looking at him. "Sometimes I wish he'd been more willing to settle down somewhere, but I knew that wasn't him from the first time I met him. There was always a sense of adventure about him that not many people had. There was also a sense of ambition that ultimately led to some bad news, but I don't like to think about that part."

Jayden pulled her to him and kissed her on the top of her head. Morgan smiled and put her arms around him, grateful he was still there.

"Do you ever wish you'd not met me? I know it's hard for you to share your life with someone else, given all that's happened."

"No. I don't think I've ever wished that, even when your snarky butt sasses me all day." They laughed together, and she nestled closer to him. "Yeah, I sure missed moments like this for the past year or so. Being single can be a blessing and a curse. I'm glad you changed my mind on the whole dating thing, although I think this whole endeavor has probably been the craziest first date I've ever been on."

"Not me," Jayden said, sniffing. "I make a point to know a girl really well by sharing magic, blowing stuff up, and ultimately almost dying with her before I think we can get to the next stage. I think everything else is just a precursor to warm us up."

Morgan smiled and playfully punched him in the stomach.

As they made it back to camp, Sibyl was tending to the wounded. "I guess that's my cue," Jayden said and headed toward his stash of herbs. He began to rifle through them, pulling out several and rushing to those with serious injuries.

Morgan sauntered over to Brenna and Alaina, still engrossed in helping their mates fully recover. "What should we do?" she asked, sitting behind them.

Brenna turned and gazed into the distance. "I think we should put him in the ground, you know, as a sort of burial. I'd hate for someone to come across him out there in the woods. Who knows what a little bit of magic could do, and I think he's probably best left alone."

Morgan nodded absentmindedly. It seemed only fitting to put him in the ground after all these years. He needed a final resting place away from prying eyes.

"I see that Noah has nearly recovered," Morgan said, gesturing in his direction.

"Nearly," Brenna agreed, turning back to him. "I don't know that the magic pierced his heart, but it certainly came close. Good thing he's strong. I don't know if I could have saved him if he had been anyone else. It takes a true heart to ward off the evil in this world."

Morgan stood abruptly and strode to Jayden. "Come on," she said. "We're going to do something about the body."

"But... I... injured people... in the middle of some-thing... Fine." He stood, giving a bag of sage to another of the witches, who took it questioningly. "Just hold it until I get back, I guess. I don't really know what this is about."

Morgan pulled him up, and he stood awkwardly. As they walked in the woods, Morgan stopped him and pulled him aside, kissing him passionately. After a moment, she let him go and continued to walk.

"You just keep going. I'm never really sure where I am with you."

She didn't respond, still trudging through the forest, her mind in a jumble. When they reached the stone statue of Zachariah—still curled on the ground, his eyes forever open in a stare—she conjured two shovels and handed one to Jayden. "We're going to bury him."

"I'm no expert," he said, "but wouldn't magic make this a lot easier?"

"Sure, it would," Morgan said, already beginning to dig, "but that's not the point of this. It's not like burying a regular stone. This means something to me, even if he tried to have me killed. It's closure, like burying the man he used to be."

They spent several hours digging in silence. After the hole had reached more than ten feet deep, Jayden jumped out of it, wiped his brow, and leaned on his shovel. "Would you like me to put him in, too?" he asked, out of breath.

"Nah, I'll do that." Morgan stood the stone on its end and pushed it unceremoniously into the pit.

"That was sort of anticlimactic to what I thought you were going to do."

"Huh?" she said, not really paying attention.

"Well, I mean, you had this huge story about wanting to bury the man he was and all that, and you just shoved him into the hole. I thought you'd, I don't know, lower him softly in or something like that."

"Well, he did try to kill me. I think I've done my good deed for the day."

Still breathing through his mouth, Jayden curled his lip in confusion then shrugged. "You certainly are a strange person, I'll give you that."

Morgan shrugged, too, and then began to fill the hole. After covering the body, she patted it with the shovel. "All set. I'd say that's good enough for now."

"Don't you think someone will notice some fresh soil on the ground? I mean, as long as we're pointing things out."

Morgan looked up. The trees around them were in tatters. Branches hanging only by bark, and the earth were so badly torn that someone might have suspected that there was some sort of natural disaster. "I think it'll be okay."

"So, what are you thinking now?" he asked as they slowly walked back to camp. "You've been doing the same thing for 300 years. You need a new hobby."

"I was thinking of opening an academy. You know, for the needy."

"I'm sorry; you want to open a hobo academy?"

"What?"

"Well, that's what I think of when you talk about the needy. And I've got to tell you, we are hardly the pair to start doing something like that. I mean, we bathe in the creek for heaven's sake."

Morgan rolled her eyes. "No, more like an academy for people who feel persecuted for their magic. A place where people can feel at home to experiment with some of the most beautiful parts of themselves."

"You are a bit of a sap," Jayden said, rubbing her head.

"Be that as it may," Morgan said through giggles, "I think I'd like to help the next generation of witches become fine people, not like Zachariah."

"Well, that's noble."

When they finally made it to camp, Caleb and Noah were both sitting. They waved as Jayden and Morgan came into view, and both her sisters turned to smile in return.

"So, what now?" Morgan inquired as she drew closer. "You two were gone for an awfully long time. Are you just going to disappear on me again? Or do you plan on staying?"

Brenna gave a sideways glance at Alaina. "I've rather become accustomed to indoor plumbing and comfortable beds. I don't know how long I could stay in a tent without going a little crazy."

"You're right," Morgan agreed. "A feather bed would really be nice."

Both Alaina and Brenna stared. After a moment, Brenna said, "You do know that mattresses are made out of foam and stuff now, right?"

"Yeah, of course. I mean, that totally makes sense." As an aside, she turned to Jayden. "What is foam?"

"I hardly remember," he replied. "You've kept me in a crappy cot for pretty much my whole life. If you wanted me to learn something about the outside world, you might have sent me out a time or two. I'm not always at your beck and call, you know."

She elbowed him in the gut, and he heaved out a snort.

"I think I can sacrifice the woods if you two agree to come teach at the academy I want to start here."

"An academy? You? Teaching?" Alaina scoffed.

Caleb hit her lightly on the back of the head. "Why are you so mean? You don't have to be a complete fool all the time." Alaina shot him a glare, but he refused to back down, sticking out his tongue.

She smiled in spite of herself. "I think I might stay around, just to keep people in line, you know. You have a rotten tendency to connect with rocks, let alone a school of willful witches."

"Do I detect a compliment in there?" Morgan asked with a half-smile.

"Of course not." Alaina turned back to Caleb, reverting to her glass-like demeanor.

"I think it's a fine idea," Noah pitched in. "I've been telling Brenna for a long time that we need to settle down somewhere where we can focus on other people instead of stuck in the middle of nowhere."

"It's your fault," Alaina cut in. "You and the ice queen could have moved to a warmer climate before."

"I'm actually more concerned about you," Brenna said, putting her hand on Morgan's knee. "We still haven't found a fix for your problem with your immortality. We have to recast the spell and put what is in Jayden back in you. And if we don't do it soon, we may miss our window as your magic connection is solidifying all the time."

Morgan looked at Jayden then. He stood tall, though his eyes were downcast. She could tell from his thoughts that he was reluctant to give up what he had. Not only when it came to magic, but when it came to understanding each other's thoughts and feelings. It was a kind of adrenaline rush to peer into someone else's mind and share their memories.

"Jayden, what do you think?"

He glanced up at her in shock, seemingly surprised that she had asked him about it at all. After all, it was her magic. He had only been there to take part of the burden of healing.

"I can't say that I have much of an opinion on the subject."

"What do you mean?"

"Well," he said rather sheepishly. "I love sharing what you have. Becoming a part of you has been one of the best experiences of my life. Sharing who I am and becoming a new person with you has been a unique opportunity, to say the least. But I can't impose what I feel on you. It is your magic, and they are your thoughts."

Morgan felt a wave of compassion sweep over her, and she smiled. "You don't think you have much of a place in my life anymore, do you?"

"I suppose I do, but how long can that last with immortality? Either I'll be killed young or grow to old age, and you'll stay the same beautifully young self. I can't ask you to give up so much for me."

"You don't have to." Morgan turned to him and wrapped her arms around him, laying her head on his shoulder. "I think I've made my decision.

"Brenna," she said, without looking over. "Will you marry us?"

A whoop sounded from in beside them, and everyone began to cheer and clap.

"Are you sure?" Jayden said it under his breath so only she could hear.

"I think I've lived long enough," she said and reached up to kiss him, her foot fluttering upward.

Other Books by Renee Joiner

About the Author

Renee Joiner has been in love with the supernatural for longer than she can remember, so it is no surprise that she is an author of paranormal urban fantasy. Although she discovered her passion for writing when she was only twelve years old, she didn't make her writing debut until many years into the future. Adventurous and fun-loving, she enjoys traveling to new places, exploring new sights and meeting new people. Thus, she delights in creating fantastical worlds that are sure to give her readers an escape from the real world while simultaneously providing thrilling entertainment.

Besides her special knack for writing, you'll also find a passion for metaphysics spirituality which she has been nurturing for over four decades. Renee hails from New York and currently resides with her husband in their empty nest—unless you count their three adorable fur babies—in Florida. She enjoys adding to her sea of knowledge and thus spends her free time learning new things.

To find out more about Renee Joiner, feel free to visit her **official website**.

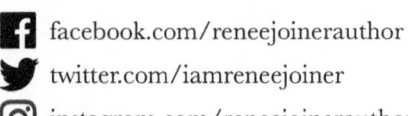

facebook.com/reneejoinerauthor

twitter.com/iamreneejoiner

instagram.com/reneejoinerauthor

Thank You..

Thank you for reading my book!
I really appreciate all of your feedback and I love to hear what you have to say. Please leave your review at your favorite retailer!